...then i met my sister

...then i met my sister

Christine Hurley Deriso

flux™

Woodbury, Minnesota

First Edition
First Printing, 2011

Cover design by Lisa Novak
Cover images: photo of woman © Photographer's Choice/PunchStock
heart illustration © iStockphoto.com/Transfuchsian

Flux, an imprint of Llewellyn Worldwide Ltd.

Library of Congress Cataloging-in-Publication Data
Deriso, Christine Hurley, 1961–
Then I met my sister / Christine Hurley Deriso.—1st ed.
p. cm.
Summary: Summer Stetson has always lived in the shadow of her dead sister, knowing she can never measure up in any way, but on her seventeenth birthday her aunt gives her Shannon's diary, which reveals painful but liberating truths about Summer's family and herself.
ISBN 978-0-7387-2581-9
[1. Sisters—Fiction. 2. Family problems—Fiction. 3. Death—Fiction. 4. Self-Actualization (Psychology)—Fiction. 5. Diaries—Fiction.] I. Title.
PZ7.D4427The 2011
[Fic]—dc22

2010045239

Flux
Llewellyn Worldwide Ltd.
2143 Wooddale Drive
Woodbury, MN 55125-2989
www.fluxnow.com

Printed in the United States of America

To Anne and Cecilia, who have always
smoothed my path. I love my sisters so.

One

"Your mom."

Gibs nods toward the audience and I follow his gaze.

Mom is sitting next to Leah Rollins' mother in the middle of the packed auditorium. They chat discreetly, leaning toward each other and holding Chapel Heights High School Honors Day programs over their mouths. Mom clings to the fantasy that Leah Rollins and I are still best friends (Leah cut me loose in ninth grade), and is no doubt telling Leah's mother that we girls just *have* to get together soon.

As she inspects our eleventh-grade class, seated on the stage for this portion of the program, Mom's eye catches mine. She waves, her cupped hand held close to her chest as her manicured fingertips flutter.

Gibs has met Mom only a couple of times, but she's

easy to spot in a crowd: trim figure, tailored suit, sleek blond hair, bright blue eyes, fake bronzed tan. At age fifty-seven, she's older than most of my classmates' parents, but her high-maintenance grooming habits have served her well. The only thing that makes her look old is her expression. Her eyes are anxious, her smile tight.

"Why is she here?" Gibs whispers, then catches himself. "I mean..."

But there's no way to recover, so he repeats the question. "Why *is* she here?"

"Because she's a lunatic."

The principal's voice drones on, and pretty soon, he's calling Gibs' name for the zillionth time.

"Highest grade point average in history—Gibson Brown."

Gibs tosses me an apologetic glance and heads toward the center of the stage to accept his certificate, his brown ponytail bobbing with every lanky step. Then he heads back to his seat, loosens his tie, and adds the certificate to the pile accumulating under his seat.

"Highest grade point average in *history*, Gibs?" I whisper, pushing a lock of long blond hair behind my ear. "You mean no one in history has ever made a higher grade point average than you? Pretty impressive."

He tosses me a smirk. "The subject, Summer," he tells me. "History the *subject*."

The principal is droning on again. "Highest grade point average in honors English—Gibson Brown."

The audience chuckles when Gibs has to head right back

to the center of the stage. "Perhaps Gibson and I should trade places," the principal wisecracks. More laughter.

Gibs finally gets to catch his breath when the principal moves on to Best Effort Awards. It seems logical that Gibs' top marks attest to excellent effort, but no, Best Effort Awards go to the losers who squeak by with C's and make their teachers happy by keeping their mouths shut in class.

I squeak by with C's but don't keep my mouth shut in class, so no Best Effort Awards for me.

Which brings us back to Gibs' question: why *is* my mother here?

It was the source of a heated argument at breakfast:

"So the Honors Day ceremony starts at nine, right, Summer?"

I eyed my mother suspiciously while she washed dishes at the sink.

"Why do you ask?"

"Because I'm going, of course!"

The fork clanged as it dropped from my fingers onto my plate. "And why might that be?"

"Oh, Summer. Pipe down and finish your breakfast."

"Hate to disappoint you, Mom, but I'm coming up dry."

Mom avoided eye contact, just kept scrubbing china until it whistled as she told me she'd be there to support *all* the students, including me, for effort if nothing else.

So my shutout in the Best Effort categories must hit her particularly hard.

I should feel guilty. God knows *Mom* deserves a Best

Effort Award for all the nagging, cajoling, bribing, and pleading she does to try to nudge me into honor student status.

Gibs thinks my underachievement is passive-aggressive, and I'm cool with that theory since it's more flattering than the truth, which is that I'm lazy.

Plus awful at math. I'm energetically bad at math. I try, if for no other reason than to avoid my mom's pinched looks as I struggle through homework, to solve the damn problems. I just can't, which makes Gibs' passive-aggressive theory even more appealing.

The ceremony finally concludes with the principal's observation about how great we *all* are, award or no award, but greatness notwithstanding, we award-deficient types should aspire to collect our own little stack of papers at next year's ceremony. Motivational speeches always have the opposite effect on me.

Priscilla Pratt strikes up a hearty version of Beethoven's *Ode to Joy* for a piano recessional, and Mom vigorously seeks out eye contact with me, pointing emphatically to Priscilla.

She's mouthing words I can't make out but nevertheless understand perfectly. Priscilla and I used to carpool to piano lessons. But alas, I was a piano lesson dropout, and here's Priscilla, entertaining the throngs with her hard-earned virtuosity. *She* practiced her scales. Mom is mouthing something along those lines.

I nod. *Yes, Mom. Priscilla's a keeper.*

But does she have to bang the keys so hard? It's jangling, what with those tinny, vibrating chords bouncing off the auditorium walls like shrapnel.

"Good thing Beethoven was deaf, or he'd be rolling over in his grave," I mutter to Gibs as we take baby steps in the recessional line off the stage.

"The major religions would argue that God restores all the senses after death," Gibs says over his shoulder.

"Then Beethoven is suffering right now, which is very unheaven-like."

"SSSHHH!"

Mrs. Treat's shushes are always louder than whatever conversation she's shushing, making all eyes fall on her. She gratuitously nudges our elbows onward, as if we'd be roaming aimlessly without her cool plump arm guiding us off the stage. When she scowls (and she's scowling now at me), she looks like Mao Tse-tung. Mom will manage to seek her out during the reception and gush about what a great job she's done putting together this wonderful assembly.

We filter into the auditorium lobby (joylessly, I might add, Priscilla's and Beethoven's best efforts notwithstanding), where I see Mom's head bobbing about in search of me. She's standing next to Leah Rollins' mother, who starts flapping her Honors Day program in the air when she spots me. I groan as the two moms weave their way through the crowd in my direction.

"Summer ...!" Leah's mom says. It sounds like the first word of a sentence, but what else is she going to say, what with Leah and me being history and my dismal showing in Honors Day. So that's all she says.

"Hi, Mrs. Rollins."

"Wasn't Leah *wonderful*?" Mom coos, as if we just saw her on Broadway.

Mrs. Rollins waves away the compliment, then says, "She didn't get nearly as many awards as I'd hoped." Then she spots Gibs, who is hovering nervously by my side. "Who stands a chance when *this* fellow is in the class?"

Truly, Gibs totally blew the curve when he transferred to Chapel Heights earlier in the year. His nudging Leah Rollins from the top of the class ranking must piss off Mrs. Rollins mightily.

"Yes, young man, you certainly were impressive," Mom says to Gibs. The only thing distracting her from his ponytail is his fist full of awards.

"Thanks," he says shyly.

"Summer, aren't you going to introduce us to your friend?" Mom asks.

"It's Gibs," I say. "Gibson Brown. You've met."

"Oh? When?"

"A couple of times," I say testily. "The PTA breakfast *five days ago*, for one."

That was in the ponytail-distracting days, before Mom knew he was brilliant.

"*You* know, Susanne," Mrs. Rollins prods. "His family moved here from Cleveland in the middle of the school year. His father is a Very Prestigious Surgeon."

Ponytail or no ponytail, Gibs' cachet has just shot through the friggin' roof.

"Mmmmm," Mom says, raising a single and perfectly groomed eyebrow.

"Well, Gibson, keep up the good work," Mrs. Rollins says, by which she means go to hell.

"Barbara, we just *have* to get our girls together soon," Mom tells her.

"Oh, speaking of Leah," Mrs. Rollins replies, teetering on her tiptoes as she peers deeper into the crowd, "there she is with all her friends." She sucks in her breath after the last word, but it's too late, so she flashes me a guilty look. I smile gamely.

"Better run," she says, blushing, then heads in Leah's direction. Mom's gaze follows her wistfully, then turns back to Gibs and me.

"Well," she says. "I'm very proud of you both."

I guess she's claimed Gibs now as her own.

Thank God she has something to be happy about.

Two

"Whatcha doin'?"

Catch the cadence: *Whatcha doin'*. It's Mom trying to sound casual. I guess she figures it's less off-putting than *Why in God's name are you frittering your life away on that computer?*

What I'm *doin'* is what I always do when Mom walks in when I'm on the computer: X-ing out the screen. I usually don't have any particularly compelling reason to do this; it's just a habit. The fact that it drives Mom crazy is a bonus. She insists that we keep the computer in "a central location" (our den), so I have no privacy when I'm IM-ing or playing solitaire or doing other computer-related things that constitute frittering my life away. Dad went to bat for me once, a few years ago, saying I should have my own laptop or we should at least put the computer in a more private place, but Mom stopped him cold by saying, "Hello? *Child molesters*?!?" Which, let's face it, tends to have a chilling effect on any conversation.

"Hmmm?" Mom persists when I don't answer her *whatcha doin'* question, which I naively assumed was rhetorical. She bends down to gaze at a blank computer screen.

"Nothing." I mindlessly tap a key, waiting for her to walk away so I can finish my conversation with Gibs.

She clucks her tongue, which usually means she's about to walk out, only to jerk her head back in my direction after a few steps to let me know I'm putting nothing past her, she's always watching, she's ever vigilant about the centrally located computer, she's on to those child molesters, she's a *good* parent. But instead, she sits down in the recliner by the computer. The chair faces the television set, not the computer, but she swivels to face the back of my head and the blank computer screen.

I tilt my head slightly in her direction, giving her a sideways glance.

"Ya need something, Mom?"

"I need your attention," she snaps. The whole *watcha doin'* folksiness is apparently history.

I roll my eyes while I have the chance, then turn around to face her.

"Yep," I volunteer tersely.

"Your friend, Gibson, certainly distinguished himself in the Honors Day ceremony," Mom says.

I nod. "Yeah. He's great. Actually, he's coming over after

dinner to help me study for my history final. Hope that's okay."

Mom's face brightens. "Well, of course. That's a wonderful idea. Summer, that's the kind of thing you should be doing more of. Maybe if you'd started that earlier in the school year... I mean, here it is, the middle of May, with the school year almost over, and..."

"But better late than never, right?" A tight smile is glued to my face.

"Summer, I won't lie," Mom says archly. "I know school has never been your strong suit, but it was a little difficult sitting through another Honors Day ceremony with such... disappointing results."

My smile fades. "I told you not to come. You knew I wasn't winning anything."

Anger flashes in Mom's steel-blue eyes. "You'll be a senior next year," she says in a frosty tone. "Everything you're doing now is paving the way for your future. You should be making A's, and logging volunteer hours, and doing extra-credit projects in school, and..." She sighs aggrievedly. "You know, by the time Shannon was your age, she..."

My withering stare stops her cold. Mom's not the only one who can pull off frosty.

"Oh, stop being so sensitive," Mom snaps. "It's not like I'm comparing the two of you, I'm just..."

I give her a minute to squirm. She's got nothing.

"I'm just pointing out," she soldiers on, "that your sister was... she was very..."

She can't come up with the next word, which is apt. The superlative says it all. Shannon was Very. I am Not.

"I don't know what you want me to do, Mom," I say. "Like you said, the school year is almost over."

Mom folds her arms and nods briskly. "I want you to turn over a new leaf," she replies. "I want you to ask your teachers for some extra-credit assignments this summer. I want you to buckle down next year and be the straight-A student we both know you can be. I want you to do some volunteer work. I want you to think about your *future*, Summer."

Which is ironic, because as far as I can tell, all Shannon ever did was think about her future. And she ended up not having one.

Whatever look I'm giving Mom is frustrating the hell out of her. She leaps out of her seat with a burst of adrenaline. "And if you *don't*," she says, pointing a manicured finger at me like a dagger, "don't think you're going to sit around here all summer doing nothing. If you can't find anything constructive to do, I'll find something *for* you."

She strides out of the room, leaving a Shalimar-scented *whoosh* in her wake. I sit there for a second, chilled by the breeze she leaves behind, then turn back to the computer.

I see real potential in sitting around here all summer doing nothing.

Three

"You have a sister?"

Gibs and I have been friends since he moved to town a few months ago; he noticed me reading Nietzsche during lunch one day at school and wondered why somebody who read Nietzsche for fun wasn't in his honors classes. He's pretty shy, but we bonded over stolen smirks during a particularly painful poetry reading at a school assembly (don't get me started on Priscilla Pratt's breathless insights regarding sunsets or Leah Rollins' groundbreaking take on the Importance of Honesty), and Gibs started inviting me to his house occasionally for guitar sessions or indie videos.

But this is his first trip to *my* house; Mom's tendency to make my friends feel like they're under FBI surveillance minimizes my invites. But she's at work now, and I really need help with my history final, so here's Gibs.

It occurs to me that it must strike him as pretty odd that I've never mentioned my sister. We've just walked past the Shannon Wall of Fame, on into the den where Shannon's life-sized watercolor portrait smiles down on us from the most prominent wall in the room

"*Had*," I say in response to his question. "I *had* a sister. She's dead."

"Oh," Gibs says. "I'm sorry."

"It's okay. I never knew her. She died before I was born. Actually, she's the *reason* I was born."

Gibs narrows his eyes, waiting to hear more, but that's really all I have to say about that. I let my backpack slide off my arms onto the carpet, unzip it, and pry out my history book. I plop on the floral overstuffed couch and start flipping pages.

"I'm really rusty on the Prussians," I say, after settling on a page.

"What do you mean, she's the reason you were born?" Gibs persists.

I shrug. "My parents were bummed when she died, so they had me. I'm their sloppy second."

Gibs pushes a stray lock of hair behind his ear and sits on the other end of the couch. "Their what?"

"Their sloppy second. Shannon was perfect, their lives were perfect, everything was perfect-perfect-perfect, then she died. And my mom thought if she got pregnant again, she'd have another perfect baby. But she had me."

I'm back to flipping pages, but Gibs sits on the other

end of the couch and kicks off his sneakers like he's settling in for details.

"How did she die?"

I squint to focus on the glossary. "Car accident."

Gibs' eyebrows knit together. "What happened?"

I look at him squarely. "Didn't I just say? A car accident. An accident involving a car."

He shakes his head impatiently. "But what *happened*?"

I sigh, toss my book to the side and hug my jeans-clad knees against my chest. "She was driving to school. It was the first day of her senior year. A dog ran in front of her...or a cat, or a squirrel...something...and she swerved and hit a tree."

Gibs stares at his fingers. "Wow." He blushes. "I'm really sorry."

I poke his arm playfully. "I didn't know her, remember? Telling me you're sorry she's dead is like telling me you're sorry Abraham Lincoln is dead. And speaking of history..." I nod toward my book.

"It's not like that at all," Gibs counters, glancing at her portrait on the wall. "She was your sister. God, you two look like twins. She's, like, a *piece* of you."

"Well, your great-great-grandfather was, like, a piece of you. But you can't miss someone you never knew."

Gibs' dark blue eyes flicker in my direction. "A sister's not like some random ancestor. Great-great grandfathers are *supposed* to be dead. Sisters aren't."

I consider his point, but mostly, I'm irritated we're talking about the subject in the first place. "I know," I say patiently. "It's very sad she died. On the other hand, if she hadn't died, I wouldn't have been born, so I wouldn't be here to talk about why you can't miss somebody you never knew, so…"

"How do you know that?" Gibs asks, his eyes now locked with mine.

"Know *what*?"

"That you wouldn't be here if she hadn't died?"

I shrug. "My parents only had me because they were so bummed about losing her."

Gibs peers past me. "Which makes you wonder…I mean, life may be totally random…but if there's some kind of grand plan, if you were meant to be here, it's like Shannon had to die to make that happen."

I huff and sit up straighter. "History. We're supposed to be studying history."

Gibs rests his chin on his fist. "But what's the point, if everything's random? Even weirder, what's the point if everything's predetermined? What good is learning about history if we don't have the power to control our own fate? Maybe you're destined to flunk history, and nothing we do can change that. Or maybe an asteroid will randomly hit the earth ten seconds from now, and none of this will matter anyway."

I grab a throw pillow and playfully bounce it over his head.

"Or maybe my history teacher will morph into a Vulcan and whisk us away on the Starship Enterprise. But on the off chance that I actually have to pass my history exam, could you please help me study?"

Gibs looks at me evenly. "So you never even think about her?"

I toss my head backward and groan. "Why do we have to talk about this?"

"You *do* think about her," Gibs deduces. "You've got to. She's your sister."

I stare at the ceiling fan and notice a strand of cobweb extending from the ceiling to one of the blades. Somehow, the strand stays intact even as the fan slowly oscillates. "I have no choice but to think about her," I tell Gibs, still staring skyward. "Especially with friends like you."

It's true. Shannon has been the backdrop of my life since the moment I was born...since the moment I was *conceived,* really. My earliest memory is of my grandma getting misty-eyed when I sat at the kitchen table threading macaroni noodles onto the tines of my fork. "Just like Shannon used to do," Grandma said in a choked voice, at which point I stopped threading the noodles and started dicing them into slivers. I thought it would make Grandma laugh, but instead she turned stern. "Eat your lunch," she scolded.

"*I'll eat my lunch*," I remember thinking, "*but I'll do it my way.*"

Our house is like a Shannon museum, featuring the Wall of Fame with its framed photos of every school picture. As you walk down the hall leading to our den, you move from toothless first-grader to stunning blonde in the course of just a few steps. The effect is like a bubble that grows larger, larger, larger until it bursts.

My school photos are on the opposite wall. Shannon never looks directly into the camera, always past it, but my eyes stare straight ahead … straight into *Shannon*, as if indicting her for being so much more fabulous. Shannon's sparkly eyes, gazing past me, are oblivious.

This year, the number of photos grew even. When Mom hung my eleventh-grade photo opposite Shannon's, perfect symmetry was achieved. My senior photo will ruin the effect. And of course, I'll have no one to bore my eyes into.

The second-story hall displays our framed certificates and plaques. *That* wall will never be symmetrical. *Shannon Elizabeth Stetson, First Place. Shannon Elizabeth Stetson, Grand Prize. Shannon Elizabeth Stetson, Perfection Personified.* Shannon outpaced me by the time she was in second grade. I don't know how there were enough hours in the day to accommodate her dancing, her cheering, her debating, her junior-achieving, her future-business-leading, her volleyball, her school honors, her vast greatness in general. You can tell at a glance that Mom had aesthetics in mind when she first started hanging Shannon's frames. In the earlier ones, she gave careful attention to placement, ensuring an equal amount of space between each frame. But as Shannon's honors accumulated, Mom's eye for decorating took a back seat to practicality, with frames squeezing ever closer together and forming cluttered new layers that eventually covered the surface like wallpaper.

The opposite wall—my wall of shame—is sad and sparse, a few honorable mentions for art or writing, a few photocopies of the same certificate every kid on the soccer team gets for showing up and having a pulse.

Having a pulse. There's that stab of guilt I get when I think too long or too hard about Shannon. I can be glib in short spurts. My conscience kicks in on longer intervals.

"You *do* think about her," Gibs' voice reverberates in my head. "You've got to. She's your sister."

But he's wrong. I don't think about her much, mostly because I don't have much to think about. True, her greatness stares me in the face every second of my life, but it's an abstract greatness, as generic and one-dimensional as the certificates on the wall. Our house may be a Shannon Museum, but my family never shares anything real about her. Did she ever adopt a stray cat? Throw a tantrum because she didn't get a Christmas present she wanted? Damned if I know. Mom and Dad can't go there.

All I really know is how she threaded her macaroni through the tines of her fork, or other little tidbits my relatives might share in hushed, reverent voices, the way they talk about saints.

But from Mom and Dad, I get nothing. The photos and certificates apparently say it all.

I remember going to the zoo with my parents when I was about five. Mom was holding my hand as we walked past the elephants, and I asked if they'd ever taken Shannon there. Her grasp turned into a death grip. My knuckles blanched as Mom gave my arm a yank and pulled me along faster. Dad scurried to keep up.

And I'd missed my chance to take a closer look at the elephants, my favorite animal.

They never did answer my question, or any others about Shannon that might come to mind.

And I stopped asking.

"Prussians," I remind Gibs, sounding testier than I intended.

"Right," Gibs agrees. "Prussians."

Four

I'm dreaming that I've fallen down a manhole and mice are nibbling on my toes.

I squeal out loud. Something really *is* nibbling on my toes.

Oh, right. It's my birthday.

I open my eyes and squint against the bright sunshine that pierces through the slits in the shutters. Mom is at the foot of my bed, smiling at me.

"Eight, nine, ten! All there."

I yank my foot away from her cool hand. This is no way to start the weekend.

"Mom, it's *Saturday*."

She walks around the bed and kisses my forehead. "You know I always have to start your birthday by counting your fingers and toes. It's a tradition … the first thing I did when you were born."

I rub my eyes sleepily. "Can't we just assume they'll all be there from one year to the next? I mean, if I severed a finger or a toe, I'd probably mention it at the time, rather than waiting for you to find out during the next birthday count."

Mom brushes hair off my forehead and smiles. "My witty, silly Summer." She gazes into my eyes. "I can't believe you're seventeen."

Her throat catches on the last word.

"Japanese tonight?" I ask, eager to change the subject.

"We have reservations at seven," Mom says, her voice firm and strong again. "Grandma and Grandpa are coming, and Aunt Nicole and Uncle Matt, and … oh, did you want to invite your friend? The surgeon's son?"

"Gibs? I dunno. I guess so. He's been helping me study for my history final, so I kinda owe him anyway. Is it okay?"

"Of course it's okay. We'd love to have him. So … are you two getting serious?"

I prop up on my elbows. "About my history final? Yes, we're very serious about it."

Mom raises an eyebrow. "You know what I mean."

Unfortunately, I do. It drives Mom crazy that I don't date. Frankly, I'd rather date amphibians than most of the guys in my school. Gibs is different, of course—smart, sweet, funny—which is what makes him such a good friend, which is why we spent the junior/senior prom watching Monty Python movies in his basement.

"We're just friends, Mom," I say.

"Hmm." Mom's *hmm* means *we'll see about that.*

Then she just keeps sitting there. Like I'm on a ventilator or something.

I flutter my eyelashes to signal that now that Mom has verified my fingers and toes are still intact, I might as well go back to sleep, considering it's seven a.m. on a Saturday. But she isn't budging.

"Well," she finally says. "Time for work."

I peer at her quizzically. "Do I have a job?"

"Oh, quit being silly. I told you Aunt Nicole needed help at the flower shop."

My jaw drops. "Uh, *not.*"

"Uh, *yes.* I distinctly remember discussing it with you."

I huff indignantly. "Was I in the room at the time? Or maybe we 'discussed' it when I was asleep? *God*, Mom." She's such a control freak.

But she's not listening to me. She's set her plan in motion, and now all she has to do is move the little chess pieces to her specifications. I'm a lowly pawn. She flutters through my room, opening blinds, pulling clothes out of my closet, patting my leg—"Up, up! Chop, chop!"—and spraying asthma-inducing air freshener for good measure.

"I'll have breakfast waiting when you get downstairs," she says briskly. "Hurry! You start at nine."

"Mother!" I finally manage to wail, but she's floating

out the door, all tip-toed lightness and swooping skirt. Control-freaking puts her in such a good mood.

I groan, make my way to the shower, come back in my room, cough away the air freshener fumes, slip on some jeans and a T-shirt, then run a brush through my hair. Mom gives my hair a look of concern at least a couple of times a day, sometimes holding up a strand, studying it as if it were a lab specimen, then letting it fall limply back into place. My hair is "fine-textured," she's explained to me patiently, making it sound like a disease diagnosis, and requires "extra care" that I tragically can't muster the motivation to give it. So I grow it long and swish it in her direction at every opportunity.

I walk downstairs and join Mom and Dad in the kitchen. Mom glances at me, winces, then turns back to the eggs on the stove.

"Happy birthday, honey," Dad says without looking up from the newspaper. "Any special plans for the day?"

"Other than slave labor?" I ask, joining him at the table.

"Summer got a job in Aunt Nicole's flower shop," Mom says, bizarrely insinuating I had a hand in my fate.

"Mmmmmm," Dad says. He functions in this household on a strictly need-to-know basis.

"Need some help with your hair?" Mom asks as she spoons eggs onto my plate. "A blow-dryer would give it some body."

"What am I supposed to do at the flower shop?" I ask, stabbing my eggs with a fork.

"Whatever Aunt Nicole asks you to do," Mom replies.

"Yeah, what exactly might that … entail?" I'm envisioning some poor bride carrying a handful of dandelions and wild onion greens down the aisle after I'm tasked with making her bouquet.

"I don't know," Mom murmurs, adding more eggs to my plate. "Maybe she'll have you keep the books or something."

"Keep the books."

"Don't be sarcastic, Summer."

I sigh. "All I did is repeat what you said."

"I'm sure Aunt Nicole will put you to work in whatever way you can be helpful. You'll learn some new skills, earn a little spending money. It'll be great."

Dad turns toward Mom. "Does she have to start on her birthday?"

"Well, it's not like she had any elaborate plans," Mom sniffs.

Touché. No statewide literary meets, drill team competitions, or dressy-casual birthday teas for *me* today.

Dad winks at me. "Sometimes the best plans are *no* plans."

Mom clangs dishes noisily behind me. Dad never gets with the program. I love that about him.

————

"Bless you."

"Thanks," I tell Aunt Nic, wiping a watery eye.

I've sneezed, like, eighty times since I walked into the flower shop. I've been here a million times before, but there's something about being elbow-deep in amaranthus that wages war on my immune system. Where the hell are the "books" I was supposed to keep?

I've been in the back of the shop all morning, lugging flowers from a refrigerator to a work table, wiping the dirt off my arms as I drop a load, so Aunt Nic can pin the flowers onto a wreath or stuff them into a vase.

"We'll have to keep you stocked up with allergy medicine," Aunt Nic says, grabbing a bunch of peach-colored roses from my thorn-pricked arms.

Darn. I was hoping she'd say, "We'll have to keep you far, far away from this death trap."

The bell dings as a customer opens the door and calls, "Helloooo!"

"Want me to go wait on her?" I ask.

Aunt Nic surveys me hastily, then shakes her head. She's much less uptight than Mom, but I guess my scratched-up arms, watery eyes, and dirt-smudged clothes don't exactly scream *customer service*. She gives me a quick smile and walks out to greet the customer.

They begin a sing-song conversation—everybody who walks into a flower shop is apparently in a pretty decent mood—and I grab my cell phone to call Gibs.

"Hello?"

"I'm being held hostage in—ah-*choo*—my aunt's flower shop."

"Bummer. I'm painting my parents' bedroom."

Damn. Gibs can always one-up me.

"Mom is making me work here," I say. "I got, like, fifteen minutes' notice this morning that I was starting today. My *birthday*."

"Today's your birthday?"

"Yeah."

"Happy birthday."

"Thanks. Wanna eat Japanese tonight with my family?"

"Um … yeah. You sure?"

Ah-*choo*. "Yeah. Mom's your biggest fan now that she's found out you're brilliant."

"She won't be expecting me to recite poetry or explain algorithms or anything, will she?"

"Maybe. Better come prepared. My house at six?"

"Sure, and …"

Ah-*choo*.

"… thanks."

Aunt Nic rejoins me in the back room as I stick my cell phone back in my pocket.

"Hey, you're on for Japanese tonight, aren't you?" I ask her.

"Sure. Your treat?"

I wrinkle my nose. "I'm gonna have to spend all my paycheck on allergy medicine."

She pauses, weaves her eyebrows together, and nods her head toward a rumpled plaid loveseat. "Let's sit down for a sec."

I squint at her quizzically, but she's already headed for the sofa. I follow her and, as I sit down, I notice she's carrying a brown paper bag. She sits beside me, holding the bag on her lap.

"Um…" Aunt Nic says haltingly, "Uncle Matt and I will give you your birthday present at the restaurant tonight. But there's something else I thought you might like to have."

"What is it?" I strain to peek into the bag.

Aunt Nic pauses. She looks like she's tossing words around in her head, giving them a test run before saying them out loud. Finally, she hands me the bag. "Happy birthday, honey." Her voice trembles.

"What is *up*?" I ask her, but I'm already reaching inside the bag rather than waiting for an answer. I pull out a book. It's bound in plump lavender fabric. It's faded and, even with no writing on the cover, it looks dated.

"Honey." Aunt Nic grabs my hands, loosening the book from my grip as it lands on my lap with a dull thud.

"Yes?"

"You don't have to read this if you don't want to."

I glance down at the book, suddenly acutely curious. Every English teacher should preface a literature assignment this way: "You don't have to read this if you don't want to." The assignment would become downright irresistible.

"What is it?"

Aunt Nic grows paler. She opens her mouth, closes it, opens it again. "Your sister kept a journal the last summer of her life."

The book feels heavier on my lap.

I search Aunt Nic's gray eyes. "Like... 'I lost five pounds this week'? That sort of thing?"

She manages a smile. "I'm sure there's some of that in there. But there's more, too."

"You read it?" What a stupid question. Of course she read it.

But Aunt Nic shakes her head. "I've picked it up a thousand times through the years. But... it wasn't meant for my eyes. Shannon wouldn't have wanted me to read it. But I have the feeling she might have wanted to share it with her sister."

Her sister. It's weird; I've always thought of Shannon as *my* sister (the story of my life), but I've never thought of myself as *her* sister.

I touch the book gingerly.

"You don't have to read it," Aunt Nic repeats firmly. "Or, I don't know, maybe you'll start it, then want to put it away... like I did. The important thing to know is that the choice is yours."

I grip the book tightly. "Why wouldn't I want to read it?"

Aunt Nic shrugs. "I know you've always felt like you were in Shannon's shadow in some way. So you might prefer to leave the past in the past." She takes a deep breath. "But the fact is, this journal *does* exist. I can't deny you the chance to get to know your sister better, if that's what you want to do."

I cock my head. "I live in a Shannon shrine, remember? I know everything."

Aunt Nic's eyes sparkle through a thin veil of tears. "No, you don't."

I shiver a little. "You're weirding me out. Was she a closet vampire or something?"

Aunt Nic smiles and her eyes soften. "Not that I know of. But she was a real person, you know."

"I kinda thought that went without saying. Was I supposed to think she was a superhero?"

I expect her to laugh... I *want* her to laugh... but Aunt Nic leans closer and looks more serious than ever. "If you want to learn more about your sister, here's your chance."

My eyes flicker from her face to the journal and back again.

"Why do *you* have her journal?"

Aunt Nic takes a deep breath. "After Shannon died, I helped your mom go through her things. We didn't do it right away; for months, she left everything just the way it was. But when she started to get your nursery ready, she knew it was time."

Aunt Nic squeezes her eyes shut and a tear inches down her cheek. "Anyway, I found this. Shannon kept it hidden in her room. Your mom was somewhere else in the house when I spotted it. I started to call out for her, but when I opened it and started reading it..."

"Yes?"

She shrugs. "I just couldn't show it to her. Maybe I should have. I just... couldn't."

The bell on the front door dings. I jump, startled. "Helloooo!" a customer calls.

Aunt Nic inhales deeply, dabs her moist eyes, and kisses me on the cheek.

"The choice is yours," she says. "Read it if you want, ask me questions if you want, never mention it again if you want…whatever you think. I wouldn't be giving this to you if I didn't trust your judgment, Summer. You're a smart cookie."

She stands up, but I'm still frozen in my chair, clutching the journal as if it were the Holy Grail.

Then she winks at me. "And hey, knock off for the day. It's your birthday, for crying out loud." She walks up front to greet the customer, leaving me alone.

Alone with my sister.

Five

I pull a brush through my hair and glance at my watch impatiently. Where's Gibs?

I've asked him to come over an hour before we're due at the Japanese restaurant, and he's late. Well, not late. He still has another six minutes to get here on time. But it feels late.

I've moped around all afternoon, lying on my bed and gazing at the same spot in my Spanish book until I got bored enough to move to the den and flick channels mindlessly. Then on to the basement. Then back to my bedroom.

It's the journal. My head is consumed with a faded lavender book and the black Bic ink that fills its pages.

I put Shannon's journal on my dresser after I got home from the flower shop. Well, not right away. Initially, I intended to devour the whole thing in one sitting. When I got to my bedroom, I opened it to the first page but never focused my eyes. I flipped a few pages, but my eyes kept skittering away. What was my problem? Maybe this was the same feeling that had kept Aunt Nic from reading it. But how had she resisted? How am *I* resisting?

And where the hell is Gibs?

I hear Mom's sing-song voice at the bottom of the stairs. She must have seen Gibs coming up the driveway and opened the door before he could ring the bell. She's welcoming him in the foyer, complimenting his shirt. He's unusually neat for a guy with a ponytail. Like the suit during Honors Day. I bet his mom didn't even have to talk him into it.

I walk downstairs and give him a peace sign. He's wearing an Oxford shirt, unbuttoned at the collar and tucked into khaki pants. Only Gibs can manage to look preppie and boho at the same time. His face broadens into a shy, sweet smile. God, he looks cute. But it'll be another five years or so before Gibs figures out that girls dig his smile. I totally get that, so I don't waste my time even considering a crush.

He clears his throat and wishes me a happy birthday.

"Thanks."

"Doesn't Gibson look nice," Mom says, surveying my faded jeans, flip-flops and hooded sweatshirt to drive home the comparison.

"Mmmm." I nod toward the stairs. "Basement?" I say to Gibs.

"Yes!" Mom says. "Why don't you two go down to the

basement and enjoy some TV for a while? We don't have to leave for another forty-five minutes. You want some popcorn?"

I remind her that we'll soon be eating a football field of rice, along with several tons of chopped steak, shrimp and veggies. No wonder the Japanese are so skinny. They send us all their food.

I pull my hair out from under my sweatshirt as Gibs follows me down the basement stairs. We plop on the brown tweed sofa. I glance at him from the corner of my eye as he settles against the armrest.

I hug a throw pillow against my chest. "I already got one of my birthday presents," I say, aiming for nonchalant. "My Aunt Nic gave me this ... gift."

He nods politely. "Yeah?"

"Yeah."

Gibs raises his eyebrows, prodding me along.

Oh, jeez, why be coy?

"My sister kept a journal the summer before she died," I say. "My aunt gave it to me today. She said, you know, 'Read it if you want to, don't read it if you don't want to,' so I figure ..."

Gibs' doe-shaped eyes are locked with mine. "Your aunt is just now telling you about it?"

"Yeah. Who would figure—my aunt the florist, woman of mystery." I finger my chin. "You think I should read it?"

Gibs considers my question.

"Yeah," he says. "I totally think you should read it."

I nod. "Yeah, that's what I was thinking."

Gibs shakes his head. "Why are we having this conversation? Why is this even an issue? Who could suddenly be presented with their dead sister's journal and not read it?"

"You'd think, right?" I say earnestly, leaning closer to him. "When my aunt gave it to me, I thought, 'I'll lie on my bed for the next four hours reading it cover to cover.' But it didn't happen."

Gibs looks mystified. "Why not?"

"I don't know. But I *should*. I should totally read it … right?"

Gibs leans into his elbows. "What's making this a trick question?"

I sigh and toss my head backward. "I dunno. I'm kinda creeped out."

Gibs is silent, then says quietly, "I'll read it with you if you want."

The sweetness of the gesture catches in my throat. I'll seriously have to track Gibs down five years from now.

"Thanks, but … I don't think that's the solution. I think I have to get inside her head. By myself. You know?"

"Mmm. Don't be creeped out. It'll be okay. Maybe it's filled with recipes, or bad poetry like Priscilla Pratt's."

His eyes flicker toward mine for a post-facto sensitivity check.

"That's kinda what I was expecting," I say. "But I skimmed it, and … Gibs, it's like *War and Peace* or something. Whatever was going on in my sister's head that summer was weighing on her like a ton of bricks."

"Then you have to read it. It'll weigh on *you* like a ton of bricks if you don't. Just take it slow, I guess."

I nibble a fingernail and stare into space. "What if I find out more than I want to know?"

Gibs shrugs. "Then … you'll know. It's like science. Not knowing doesn't make it not so. If there's something to know, you should know."

He studies my expression for a moment. "Read it," he says simply. "Or stick it in the bottom of your sock drawer and forget about it. Me? I'd read it."

We hear footsteps coming down the stairs, and in walks Mom with a bowl of popcorn.

"Gibson looked hungry," she murmurs, placing the bowl on the oak coffee table.

I wrinkle my nose.

"Mom, why don't you ask Gibson what he got me for my birthday?" I tease, and Gibs' cheeks turn fuchsia. I'm messing with him. It would never occur to him in a million years to get me a birthday present.

"What did you get her?" Mom asks brightly, and now the fuchsia drains from his face, leaving him deathly pale.

"Uh …" Gibs looks at me for a lifeline, but I just grin at him.

He flounders, grasping for words. Then I come to his rescue. "Advice," I answer. "He gave me advice for my birthday."

Mom looks puzzled, then smiles. "Isn't that nice. You must come from one of those families that gives gifts from the heart rather than material things. Things like poems or sketches."

Gibs winces.

"I think that's lovely," Mom says. "You're so sensitive, Gibson. No wonder you and Summer are such good ... friends."

She walks back upstairs and I sputter with laughter. Gibs buries his head in his hands. "You're brutal," he moans.

"I know, but you forgive me. Right?"

He sneaks a look at me, then stares at his hands. "I *should* have brought you a present."

I shrug. "Maybe next time. I'd love a poem. Or a sketch. Or maybe you can whip together a sculpture out of twigs ..."

He blushes again.

"You *did* give me a present, goofball," I say. "I was serious about the advice. And I plan to follow it, by the way." I absently twirl a piece of hair in my fingers. "I'm going to read Shannon's journal."

Six

My birthdays have always had weird undercurrents, but this year's are the weirdest. The Japanese dinner is full of pinched smiles and sad eyes. Yeah, it's my birthday, blah blah blah, but all that the relatives can think about is Shannon. This is the year I turn *her* age. Her last age. The age that's frozen in time. Nobody says her name out loud, but you can see it in their faces. Grandma keeps leaning in to whisper to Grandpa on her right and Aunt Nicole on her left. She finally stops after Aunt Nic shoots her a patient but firm glance. By the time the chef is making a volcano out of onion rings, I feel like I'm at a wake.

"How's school going, Summer?" Grandma asks me primly. She's that desperate for conversation.

"It's going well," Mom responds, intertwining her fingers.

"So you'll be on the honor roll this term?" Grandma asks hopefully.

Term. Such a Grandma thing to say.

"She's doing very well," Mom says, the slightest bit of crankiness seeping through the false cheer.

Dad catches the waiter's eye and points toward his empty beer bottle. Mom notices and raises an eyebrow.

"Uh, another for me, too?" Uncle Matt tells the waiter, sotto voce.

"I'd love to see your name in the paper for the honor roll," Grandma says, stubbornly perpetuating the charade that I'm playing any role in this conversation whatsoever.

"She may not have quite made the honor roll," Mom says, now undeniably testy, "but her teachers rave about how bright she is. *Next* year. That's when Summer will hit her stride academically."

Gibs is trying to catch my eye, but I resist, knowing I'll giggle uncontrollably if I look at him.

"She'll be a *senior* next year," Grandpa observes dryly, pointing out that Mom is always banking on an honor roll daughter "next year" and that the buzzer's about to sound.

The waiter comes back and hands Dad and Uncle Matt their beers. Dad takes a long swallow and looks blankly at the chef dicing vegetables in a pound of lard, which will look much more harmless when it melts.

"Shannon was always on the honor roll," Grandma says.

Aunt Nic sucks in a breath. "Mother!" she whispers.

"What?" Grandma asks defensively. "Weren't we talking about the honor roll? Is it a crime to even mention her name?"

"I'm sure the last thing Summer and Gibson want to talk about on a Saturday night is school," Mom says. The edge in her voice is now downright unmistakable. Grandma's on notice.

"Gibson," Grandpa says. "What kind of name is that?"

He's not asking Gibs, who might actually know what kind of name he has. Grandpa's addressing all of us, as if we're a committee tasked to reach a consensus on what kind of name Gibson is.

"It's a family name," Mom says decisively, then looks to Gibs for verification. "Right, Gibson?"

"Uh..." Gibs says.

"It may be a family name, but it's a last name," Grandpa says grumpily. Why Grandpa would feel grumpy—indignant, really—about the name of someone he barely knows is beyond me.

"Fred!" Grandma scolds him.

"It's a lovely name!" Mom chirps. "I admire family names. They have such presence."

Aunt Nic and I share a quick conspiratorial smile. She's only three years younger than Mom, but her easy-going personality makes her seem eons younger.

"Well, I never understood why you wanted to name Summer after a season," Grandma is saying to Mom. "Of course, it's grown on me." She looks at me and says loudly, "It's a lovely name, dear."

I smile sweetly, biting the inside of my lip to avoid exploding in laughter, particularly since Gibs keeps nudging my knee.

The chef begins tossing oversized spatulas of food onto our plates.

The food orgy has begun. The piles on our plates soon resemble earthquake debris. There's no longer any trace of that pound of lard, but it didn't exactly evaporate into thin air. I look at my food suspiciously.

"Another beer, sir?" the waiter asks Dad.

"Uh, sure," he responds, as if it would be bad manners to turn him down.

"Your last one," Mom tells him under her breath.

"So, Gibson," Grandma says, "are you and Summer an item?"

Okay, that one pushes me over the edge. I drop my head and giggle uncontrollably into my chest.

"Summer!" Mom scolds, which makes me laugh harder.

"Mother, Summer and Gibson are *friends*," Mom says, enunciating carefully.

This, too, strikes me as hilarious.

Mom pokes me in the side with her elbow. "People are staring," she says through gritted teeth.

I take a deep breath, look up and glance at Gibs, who looks like he's being prepped for brain surgery.

"Sorry," I say, then erupt into another round of giggles.

Dad takes another swig of beer, Grandma looks confused, Grandpa looks bored, and Mom shoots me daggers with her eyes.

Gibs still looks petrified, but now he looks like he's on the verge of laughter, too.

"Sorry, sorry!" I repeat. "Can you guys excuse me a minute?"

I grab Gibs' arm, and he has no choice but to follow me as I get out of my chair and head toward the front door of the restaurant.

Dusk is settling as I stagger outside, Gibs in my wake, and sit on the restaurant steps. Gibs sits beside me. We look at each other and dissolve into more laughter. After we both calm down, I impulsively kiss him on the cheek.

"I'm so glad you're here."

He smiles and waves a stray strand of hair out of his face.

"Your family is..." He struggles for an adjective.

"Exhausting? Insane? Dysfunctional?" I volunteer.

He laughs. "I was going for 'nice.'"

I peer into the setting sun and shake my head. "Nah. That one definitely doesn't make the cut."

We press our legs together to make room for a couple squeezing past us on the steps.

"They *are* nice," Gibs insists as a breeze brushes against our cheeks. "And scintillating conversationalists, I might add. I totally enjoy lengthy discourses about my name."

I wrinkle my nose at him and we laugh some more. "Can we just call you Joe from now on?" I say.

Gibs shakes his head. "Let's go with Fred. That's your grandfather's name, right? Might win me some points."

I peer into his eyes. "You're blushing," I say in a light tone. "Why are you blushing?"

Which makes him blush even more. I'm still studying his face, but he's staring at his fingers.

Might win me some points. Does Gibs think that I thought he was coming on to me? *Was* he coming on to me?

Nah. Like I said, he's just not there yet. Which is cool. I mean, the last thing I want to do is ruin a great friendship with lust. Besides, lust doesn't work out so well for me under the best of circumstances. I haven't crushed on a guy since Leah Rollins unceremoniously stole Josh DuBois from me in ninth grade.

I shudder at the thought, not because I'm still crushing on Josh DuBois (I'm not), or because I still detest Leah Rollins for her betrayal (I do, but whatever), but because that whole puerile scenario makes me want to puke.

So if I figure Gibs has another five years to go before he realizes he's totally hot, I've got at least that long to go before I have the stomach for *Josh DuBois, the Remix.*

Yep. Friendship suits me just fine.

Another couple squeezes past us, and Gibs and I huddle closer, glancing at them apologetically.

"We really should go back inside," he observes.

I take a deep breath and blow out through my mouth. "Ready for round two?" I nod toward the door.

He stands up and extends his hand. I take it and he pulls me to my feet.

"Bring it on," Gibs says.

Seven

I'm settling into bed, still stuffed from Japanese food, but I'm not turning off my light just yet.

I glance at the journal on my bedside table, pause a second, then pick it up. I take a deep breath, open it, and start thumbing through the pages.

Shannon's plump, bouncy handwriting scrolls from top to bottom, from margin to margin, page after page after page. Jesus. What exactly did she have to write about? Was she attempting a cure for cancer in between volleyball practices?

No... the random words my eyes settle on eliminate the possibility of intellectual heft, her perfect grades notwithstanding. *Cheerleading... mall... boyfriend...* Jeez. Did my sister have anything in common with me at all?

But I keep thumbing through the pages, smiling in

spite of myself. I feel … connected. I mean, Shannon wrote these very words right down the hall from where I'm lying right now. Granted, she was in a puffy pink bedroom while I'm surrounded by Death Cab posters, but still, there she was … just a few feet away. Did she hear Mom gossiping on the phone with Aunt Nic while she was writing? Was she lulled by the same hum of the dishwasher that I listen to every night? By the ancestors of the same crickets, chirping in the back yard?

A chill works its way up my spine, but a gentle chill, a cozy chill, like a familiar finger lazily grazing my back. None of Shannon's pictures or certificates have ever had this effect on me. In fact, they've had the *opposite* effect, making her soulless and one-dimensional. Her handwriting, in all its juvenile glory, is adding shades and dimensions.

A lump suddenly settles in my throat. I wish I could run down the hall and shake her awake.

Stupid. *You can't miss somebody you never knew.*

I swallow the lump, shake my head impatiently, and keep thumbing through the journal.

Like I said, most of the pages are packed with words, so when I reach a page toward the end, it's noticeable for its sparseness. Just a few words, written in heavy black ink, all capped, centered on an otherwise blank page.

I press my thumb against that page to hold it open and narrow my eyes for a closer look. At first, the words don't quite register in my brain. I still even have that same silly half-smile on my face. But then I read the words again, and the smile fades. My lips mouth the words as my eyes widen:

I want to kill myself.

I want to kill myself.
I want to kill myself.

Breathe, I remind myself as my mind keeps processing the same five words in an endless loop. I inhale, then hold my breath. *Exhale.*

I close the journal, then grab the cell phone from my bedside table and fumble over the keypad. But just as I'm about to press Gibs' number, I snap my phone shut.

What would I say? *Gibs, remember the car accident I mentioned that killed my sister? Accident being the operative word? Yeah, well, maybe not…*

Tears sting my eyes.

"Did you kill yourself, Shannon?" I whisper to nobody. "Did you drive into that tree on purpose?"

A tear rolls down my cheek. What do I really know about this sister of mine? Was her life not so perfect after all?

My head is spinning, but there's one thing I know for sure—the only way to find out is to keep reading. And the beginning, I decide, is the best place to start.

Eight

*I*turn to the first page of Shannon's journal, fluff a
pillow, sit up a little straighter in my bed, and settle
in for my first real introduction to my sister.

Thursday, June 3, 1993

*Mom gave me this book so I could "journal" this
summer. I swear to God, that's what she said. I
wonder if her book club verbed the word journal.
Gotta love Mom's book club. Gotta love Mom for
giving me a summer assignment to remind me that
I'm never quite good enough. Apparently, straight A's
in honors courses don't earn you the summer off.*

*Oops! Here I am, busting Mom's chops knowing
full well that five minutes after I put down my
journal, she'll be reading every word of it. Right,*

Mom? You've snooped around long enough to find it, right? Keep up the good work. Your PTA friends don't call you Sue the Sleuth for nothing.

I peer closer at the words and squeeze the journal's faded cloth cover. I have to remind myself that Sue the Sleuth is *my* mom, too. A book club? The PTA? Since when was Mom such a joiner? And since when did Shannon hate her? None of the certificates on the Wall of Fame tipped me off about this.

Well, Mom, the joke's on you, because you're never getting your hands on this. Kills you, doesn't it? You buy me this journal specifically so you can sniff around in my business, and what do I do? I hide it in my... well, now, that's my little secret, isn't it?

But if you DID find it, Mom (which you won't), here's a heads-up about how I plan to spend my summer:

- *I'm not breaking up with Chris.*

- *I'm not ditching Jamie.*

- *I'm done with church. I spend enough time with hypocrites in this house. (Good luck explaining the whole "daughter as heathen" development to the choir, Mom.)*

- *I'm done with Eve. I'll love her til the day I die, but I can't handle her lectures anymore. I'm sorry she's envious of my relationship with*

Chris, but that doesn't excuse the awful things she says about him. Maybe if she ever gets a boyfriend of her own, she'll finally understand (get a life, Evie!). And here's a newsflash—it's possible to be a good friend and a FUN friend at the same time (quit judging Jamie, Evie!). And while I'm at it: real friends don't pump people for information only so they can earn suck-up points by blabbing the news to parents (quit ratting me out, Evie!).

I may even dye my hair purple this summer, or get a tattoo of a water buffalo. Sorry to cramp your style, Mom, but I'm living dangerously this summer. Get used to it.

I close the journal and suck in my breath. Who *is* this person? Up until five minutes ago, Shannon had as much depth as a picture on a cereal box... a smiling, overachieving cardboard cutout. But the person who wrote this journal... this sarcastic Mom-basher... this person is a stranger. Geez, and I thought *I* was hard on Mom. Sure, she's a pain in the ass, but you gotta cut some slack for anybody who's lost a kid. Oh, right. *Shannon's* mother hadn't lost a kid. Yet.

Still, Mom thought Shannon hung the moon, and here's her daughter ripping her to shreds. Where are those odes to kittens I was expecting to find?

I gingerly reopen the journal and turn a page.

Friday, June 4, 1993

Okay, I've stopped crying now.

Granted, I jumped to conclusions, but what was I supposed to think when Chris stood me up last night? I'd gone to all the trouble of arranging a perfect alibi. Jamie, AKA "Mrs. Collins," even left a message on our answering machine reminding me of my "Youth Recycling Committee" meeting. Master stroke, if I do say so myself.

But after all that trouble, Chris was a no-show at the park. I waited there for over an hour.

I spent the rest of the night trying to call him, but he didn't answer, so I cried myself to sleep. Every time Mom knocked on my door asking what was wrong, I told her I was watching a sad movie. (I went seventeen years without telling her a single lie; now it seems like I tell her seventeen lies a day.)

Anyhow, happy ending. It was a total misunderstanding. Chris called this morning and said he thought we were supposed to meet TONIGHT, not last night. He was at his grandparents' barbecue last night. I tried to be mad at him (he's such a space cadet!) but he was so sweet when he realized how upset I was. When I told him how worried I'd been—that he could have been dead for all I knew—he said he'd rather be dead than make me worry. Awwww.

My jaw drops. I was savvier at age twelve than Shannon apparently was at age seventeen. Could she really have been as naïve as she sounded? I keep reading.

> *The upshot is that my tears are dried, Chris is alive and well, and my heart is happy.*

God. She really *was* that naïve.

> *So I'm ready for a rockin' weekend. Oh, and one more thing—I've decided I'm going to talk to Mr. Kibbits about Dad.*

Dad? *My* dad? What about our dad? I swallow hard.

> *Nobody in my family ever talks about anything that matters, and if I don't talk to somebody, my internal organs are going to explode. Thank heaven for Mr. Kibbits.*

I lie there for a good five minutes, the journal frozen in my hands. I'm staring at Shannon's words, but my eyes aren't moving. I don't know what to make of the sister I've just officially met. My ceiling fan whirs lazily and casts angular shadows on my bedroom walls.

I toss the journal aside, grab my cell phone, and text Gibs:

R U awake? Call me.

My phone rings a few seconds later.

"What's up?" Gibs asks.

I press a fingernail against my mouth. "I'm reading Shannon's journal."

"How far have you gotten?"

"Just a few pages ... a couple of entries. The first two—June third and fourth."

"What do they say?" Gibs asks, trying to suppress a yawn.

I make a split-second decision not to tell him about the suicide threat. I just can't go there now.

"Um ..." I sigh. "I don't think I can keep reading."

"Why not?"

I pull the covers closer to my chin. "This isn't stuff she intended anybody to read. I feel like a peeping Tom or something."

"But it's not like she's around to be ticked off about it," Gibs replies.

"That almost makes it worse ... to be reading her private thoughts when she's not even here to defend herself."

Gibs pauses. "So she needs to be defended?"

My eyebrows knit together. "I don't know ... kinda. She's all ... snarky. And sneaky. She was mad at Mom when she wrote it, and she sounds like some kind of spoiled princess. Nothing like the way people talk about her."

"But you just read a couple of entries," Gibs reminds me. "Maybe you just caught her in a bad mood."

"Shannon didn't have *moods*," I say testily.

Gibs laughs. "O-*kay*."

"I mean ..." I sigh, then let words tumble from my

mouth. "I don't know what I mean. This journal is making her seem like a real person. And not a particularly likable one, at least so far. I'm not sure I can handle that."

"What kind of person did you think she was?" Gibs asks cautiously.

"The kind who won awards."

"On, like, a full-time basis?"

I smile wanly. "I guess I never thought it through. In my head, Shannon was always bringing awards home and making Mom and Dad convulse in ecstasy over her fabulousness."

"Snarky sounds more interesting than that," Gibs observes reasonably.

"Yeah...but she's telling secrets, too. She says in the entry that she's going to talk to Mr. Kibbits about Dad. What about Dad? It's all just too weird."

Pause. "Whoa," Gibs finally says. "It's getting interesting."

"Interesting unless it happens to be *your* dad."

"Mr. Kibbits," Gibs says to himself. "The AP English teacher?"

"Oh. Right." I knew that name sounded familiar. AP teachers and I don't exactly travel in the same circles.

"I'll be in his Honors English Comp class next year," Gibs says. "He's in this writers' club..."

"*Club*," I interrupt him. "That's another thing. Shannon talks about my mom being in clubs, like a book club, and belonging to all kinds of groups, like the church choir and the PTA, and..."

"And?" Gibs prods.

"And since when was she such a joiner? She's totally neurotic about my schoolwork and always sucks up to my teachers, but she doesn't do *clubs*."

"But apparently she did at one time."

"Whatever." I don't know why I'm snapping.

"Anyway, Mr. Kibbits' club," Gibs continues. "They meet at the library on Sunday afternoons. I've been a few times. They talk about books and sometimes read stuff they're writing to the rest of the group."

"And?"

"And tomorrow's Sunday. We should go. We can stay afterward and ask him what your sister told him about your dad."

My stomach tightens. "How is he supposed to remember a conversation from eighteen years ago?" I ask.

"Depends on how juicy it was."

Another pause.

"Sorry," Gibs says softly.

"It's okay." I can tell Gibs anything, right? I *do* tell him anything. So why do I suddenly feel so exposed? That settles it—I'm *definitely* not mentioning the suicide threat.

"Tell ya what," Gibs says. "We'll go to the writers' club tomorrow. I'll introduce you to Mr. Kibbits, then make myself scarce so you can talk to him alone."

I open my mouth to speak, but realize my throat has tightened. Tears sting my eyes.

"Summer? Are you there?"

I nod and try to speak, but the words are still stuck in my throat.

"Summer?"

"This is all just a little...weird."

He pauses. "Are you *crying*?"

I shake my head quickly. "I'm fine."

Gibs pauses again, then says, "Maybe you're right. Maybe you should just forget the journal."

But the instant he says it, I know there's no turning back. It's like I've been strapped into the roller coaster, the ride has started, and the car is inching up the incline. I'm terrified of getting to the top and hurtling down the hill, but there's no going back.

"I'll be okay," I say, chopping the last syllable short to calm the quake in my voice.

"Just pace yourself," Gibs says. "Maybe just read a little at a time. Then it won't be a big deal. It'll just be a few minutes out of your day."

"Okay." I smile at his earnestness. "Thanks, Gibs."

"So we're on for tomorrow? I'll pick you up around three?"

Stupidly, I nod, afraid my voice will break again.

Somehow, Gibs gets that. "Around three, then," he says gently.

I nod again, and he says goodnight in the sweetest voice I've ever heard. Never in my whole life have I felt as grateful to have a friend like him.

And God knows I've never needed one more.

Nine

"Morning, honey."

Dad's face is buried behind the paper again. He's sitting at the kitchen table in a white T-shirt and flannel pajama pants, eating leftovers from the Japanese restaurant.

"Stir fry for breakfast?"

"Mmmmm," Dad says, still not looking up.

I don't know if his *mmmm* means the stir fry is good or if he's totally ignoring me. Actually, I *do* know. I join him at the table and playfully thump the paper. He puts it down and smiles, his glasses still balanced against the tip of his nose.

"Did you have a good birthday?" he asks, taking another bite of leftovers.

"Mmmmmm."

He nods. As a chemical engineer at a paper plant, Dad

is brilliant with a protractor and a calculator, but irony flies right over his head.

Shannon's words are still swimming in my head. Was she as snarky to Dad as she was to Mom, particularly considering whatever secret about him she was hiding? And what could that secret be? Dad is as predictable, and about as exciting, as the numbers he crunches on his calculator. So what could Shannon have possibly known? That he threw caution to the wind one day and read the sports section before the news?

I shudder a little. I mean, what the hell do *I* know? From the couple of journal entries I've read, Shannon is already starting to sound more like a Sylvia Plath character than a pep squad leader. What do I really know about anything, especially considering that my family is about as open and accessible as Fort Knox? Do I know them at all? Do I want to?

But I don't want to tip my hand about Shannon's journal, and I don't want to freak Dad out by going from zero to ninety, communications-wise. *(Hey, Dad, I know we've never talked about anything of substance before, but do you think Shannon committed suicide? And do you have any juicy secrets from your past that you'd like to share?)*

Still, I have to dip my toe in the water. My habit of following my family's game plan—shutting down and making nice—is why Shannon's words have gobsmacked me. I don't think the game plan will work for me anymore.

I sneak a glance at Dad. He notices and gives me a wary smile.

I take a deep breath. Okay, here goes—Introduction to Dad 101. I decide to start with what seems to be the most innocuous information I've learned from the journal.

"Did we used to go to church?" I ask Dad.

Try answering *that* question with an *mmmmmm.*

"We?" Dad asks, running a hand through his gray-flecked brown hair.

"Yeah. Our family. You and Mom…and Shannon, I guess. I don't remember ever going to church, but did we? Did *you?*"

Dad absently scatters the food on his plate with his fork. "Your mother was raised Catholic."

"I know *that.*" I don't mean to sound impatient; at least he's talking. But Grandma and Grandpa are so Catholic, their house is practically decorated in Contemporary Crucifix. Mom's being raised Catholic is virtually the only thing I already know.

Dad rests his fork on his plate. "I grew up Methodist," he says. "I converted when we married. Well, not technically. I just started going to church with your mother. We went for several years, until…"

I lean subtly closer. "Until Shannon died?"

Dad's lips tighten and he stares at his food. "I guess it was around that time that we stopped going. Your mother kind of calls the shots in those matters."

It sounds so crazy—Mom "calling the shots" about the whole family's religion—but then, Mom calls the shots about everything.

"Why did you stop going?" I ask.

Dad shifts his weight and rubs the back of his neck. "Do you *want* to go?" he asks wearily, seeming to hope against hope that the answer is no. I don't think Dad is anti-religion. He's just anti-changing-his-routine.

"I just want to know why you stopped going," I repeat.

His eyes flicker in my direction, then back toward his plate. He fiddles with his fork again. "I think you'd have to ask your mother about that."

I open my mouth, then shut it, resigned. Dad takes another bite.

I watch as he chews and dabs his mouth with a napkin. He always looks a little rumpled first thing in the morning, but he's still handsome with his square jaw and deep-set eyes. I rest my chin on my knuckles. "How'd you and Mom meet?" I blurt out, surprising even myself. I don't remember forming that question in my head.

Dad smoothes his T-shirt and clears his throat. "How did we *meet*?"

"Yeah."

He crinkles his brow. "You know the answer to that, honey."

He's burying his head in the paper again.

I thump it again. "No. I don't know."

He takes a deep breath and puts the paper aside. "Sure you do. Your mom talks about those kinds of things."

"No, she doesn't."

Nobody in my family ever talks about anything that matters.

Dad glances around the room like he's looking for an

escape hatch. "Of course she does," he says, trying not to sound irritated. "School. We met in school." He stabs a piece of chicken and pops it in his mouth.

"College, right?"

"*Yes*," he says, sounding vindicated. "I *told* you that you already knew."

I absently finger a lock of hair. "When did you see her for the first time? In a class?"

"Um … a party, I think."

I smile. "Did you like her right away? Did you think she was pretty?"

He peers into space. "I believe my roommate introduced us."

"And you asked her out that night?"

A hint of impatience flashes across Dad's face, but then, unexpectedly, his eyes soften and he smiles.

"What?" I ask him.

He blushes. "It's kind of embarrassing."

I bounce a little in my seat. "*What*?"

He holds a hand loosely over his mouth. "I wanted to ask her out, but I was too shy. I had a part-time job in the comptroller's office and I told her it was fortunate we'd happened to meet at the party, because I'd just been going through the files and there were some 'discrepancies' with her paperwork."

My jaw drops slightly. "You're the only person I've ever known to use the word 'discrepancies' in a pickup line."

Dad scowls at me playfully. "Well, it worked. She dropped by the office a couple of days later. I told her I must have confused her file with someone else's, that all of her paperwork was perfectly in order ... and the rest is history."

Mom walks in the kitchen, tightening the sash of her terrycloth robe. She gives us a little nod and heads for the coffeemaker.

"Mom," I say, "did you know Dad tricked you into seeing him again after you first met by telling you something was wrong with your college paperwork?"

"Of course," she says matter-of-factly.

"You never knew that," Dad protests.

Mom gives a little snort as she pours herself a cup of coffee.

"You *did* know," I say, more to myself than to Mom, "but it was okay, because you wanted to see him again, too?"

Dad gazes at Mom, waiting for her response. He's actually curious. I've never known him to be curious about anything other than golf before.

"Well?" I press.

Mom waves a hand dismissively through the air as she takes a sip of coffee. "This is ridiculous," she says decisively. "Randall, the grass needs cutting. Better get it done this morning, before it gets too hot."

Dad buries his head back in the paper. "Mmmmmm," he says.

"Mom, why don't you go to church anymore?" I ask her impulsively.

Her shoulders stiffen as she searches my face for a clue

about my sudden penchant for memory lane. "Do you *want* to go to church, Summer?"

"I'm just wondering why we don't," I say. "I mean, Dad says we used to. Or *you* used to. I don't remember ever going except for holidays."

"You know that you can go to church any time you'd like," Mom says defensively. "I'll take you this morning if you'd like to go."

"No, it's not that I *want* to go. I just…"

"The grass, Randall," Mom interrupts, casting me an annoyed look. "Don't forget to cut the grass this morning."

I sigh as Mom walks out of the kitchen with her coffee, her robe swooshing through the air. I stare for a second at the paper that hides Dad's head, wishing I could keep him talking and wondering if I can pull him back into the conversation.

But no. He's more than filled his word quota for the day.

The magic is gone.

Ten

So this is a library, huh?"

Gibs stops in his tracks and stares at me, jaw dropped and eyebrows arched.

"I'm kidding," I assure him.

We walk through the foyer and a security turnstile, then into the brightly lit expanse of books, computer banks, tables, chairs, and grim faces of people who spend Sunday afternoons in libraries. (Okay, so they're not all grim-faced. But they do seem awfully pale.)

"This way," Gibs says in a lowered voice, leading me past the reference desk toward a closed door. He squeaks the heavy oak door open and I follow him inside.

"…so I guess you'd say the tundra—or, more specifically, the ice—serves as a metaphor," a guy in a sports jacket and a dress shirt with an unbuttoned collar says into a microphone, leaning way too close to it. He sounds like a grocery store manager calling for cleanup in aisle six.

Gibs and I slip into seats on the back row. "He's been reading chapters of his novel at the last few meetings," Gibs whispers to me, nodding toward the guy at the podium.

About a dozen people are scattered in the other seats looking... oh, let's just face it: grim. Who other than a person without a life would spend a Sunday listening to a guy talking in a monotone about climate-related metaphors?

I shoot eye signals to Gibs to convey my concern about their loser status, but he knows me well enough not to take the bait. He stares straight ahead intently.

Someone raises a hand and asks if the shoes in the novel are also metaphors, and Grocery Store Manager responds in endless droning. My shoulders slump. I try again, unsuccessfully, to make eye contact with Gibs. I start counting polka dots on the blouse of a plump lady in front of me. Thank heaven we came toward the end of the meeting.

"You voluntarily come and listen to this stuff?" I whisper to Gibs, who shushes me with a stern expression.

"The metaphor that runs throughout my short story is fire," says Polka Dot Lady.

People nod earnestly.

"Maybe you can read your story at the next meeting," Grocery Store Manager offers congenially, and Polka Dot Lady seems excited at the prospect, though she blushes and explains that it's not quite finished yet.

"This place is death," I whisper to Gibs.

He looks stern again, but thankfully, Grocery Store Manager seems to be wrapping things up.

"As you know, we always like to adjourn with a tip of the day," he says, and I'm so excited by the word *adjourn* that I almost burst into spontaneous applause. "Today's tip concerns writers' block. If you're stuck—and who among us hasn't been—stop what you're doing, go turn the television on, watch it for fifteen minutes, then incorporate something from what you've seen into your story. Even if you edit or delete it later, the challenge should get the creative juices flowing."

"Why not hurl your TV set through your neighbor's window, watch his reaction, then incorporate *that* into your story?" I murmur to Gibs. He closes his eyes and shakes his head slowly.

People rise from their seats, make small talk, and start filing out of the room.

"That's him," Gibs says, nodding toward a trim guy in jeans who looks youthful despite his close-cropped gray hair.

As Mr. Kibbits makes his way toward the door, he spots Gibs and smiles.

"Ah, Gibson! Glad you could join us today."

He extends a hand and Gibs shakes it. "Thanks. Um…this is my friend, Summer."

Mr. Kibbits pivots toward me and shakes my hand.

"Hi," he says. "I've seen you around school. You're a rising senior, like Gibson, right?"

"Right."

"Are you taking AP English Comp next year?" he asks me.

I glance away. "Honors courses aren't really my thing."

His blue-gray eyes twinkle. "And what might your thing be?"

"That's what my mom wants to know," I say gamely, tucking a lock of blond hair behind my ear. "Can I check back with the two of you after I've figured it out?"

Mr. Kibbits chuckles as Gibs leans closer. "Can Summer have a minute of your time?" Gibs asks him.

Mr. Kibbits spreads out his hands. "Does this qualify?" he asks cheerfully.

"She wants to discuss something with you privately," Gibs explains in a lowered voice.

Mr. Kibbits smiles at me. "Care to have a seat?"

He motions toward a chair. I sit down and he sits next to me. Gibs offers a quick wave. "I'll be … checking out some books," he says, then walks out of the room with his dark ponytail bouncing lightly behind him.

I get right to the point. "I think you knew my sister. Shannon Stetson."

He smiles. "Correct."

I peer closer at him. "So you remember her?"

He nods. "Very vividly. She was a memorable person."

"And you know she was my sister?"

Mr. Kibbits nods again. "Chapel Heights is a pretty small town. Lots of people remember Shannon. Word circulated quickly when you started high school. The teachers who were there when Shannon was in school ... we kind of compare and contrast."

"Right ... " I say. Damn. Shannon's shadow follows me everywhere I go. At least the teachers are subtle about it. Most of them, anyway.

"I don't mean to make you self-conscious," Mr. Kibbits says gently. "Everything I've ever said, or ever heard said, was highly complimentary of both of you."

I swallow hard. "My aunt just gave me a journal Shannon kept the summer before she died," I say quickly. My eyes look away, then dart back to catch Mr. Kibbits' reaction. He still has the same pleasant, placid expression pasted on his face.

"I just started reading it," I continue. "She mentions you in the second entry."

He touches an index finger against his chin. "Really."

"She mentions a couple of other people, too. Chris—that was her boyfriend, I think—and Jamie. Did you know them?"

Mr. Kibbits nods. "Chris Ferguson. He still lives in town ... works on cars at Phipps' Auto Shop, I think. I've lost track of Jamie."

"Why didn't my mom like them?"

He isn't surprised by the question. "They had nothing in common with Shannon," he says, then thinks for a couple of seconds before clarifying. "As an AP teacher, I see lots of high achievers."

"And ... ?"

"Most of them have been high achievers all their lives,"

he continues. "The kind of kid who runs for Student Council year after year and breaks records selling Girl Scout cookies. That sorta thing."

"Mmmmmm," I say knowingly. That's the Shannon who's been rubbed in my face all my life.

"Some of them are just naturally high-achieving," Mr. Kibbits says, "and some are pushed by their parents to excel, excel, excel. Sometimes both."

Check and check, I say to myself.

"By the time they get to my class—their junior or senior year—a lot of them are pretty burned out," Mr. Kibbits says.

I finger a lock of hair. "Burned out?"

He nods. "Perfection is exhausting."

I never considered that. "So, Shannon was burned out?" I persist.

He weighs his words carefully. "I think so. But just temporarily, in my opinion. She was so naturally driven that she was destined to do big things in a big way. But by the time I got to know her, she was starting to question whether all her hard work was worth the effort. She was starting to question lots of things. I think that's why she started hanging with a different crowd—people like Chris and Jamie."

My eyes narrow. "Did she hate my mom?" I say it so fast I don't have time to censor myself.

He looks amused. "Don't all teenage girls hate their mothers?"

Not good enough. "*Why* did she hate her?" I suddenly

feel fearless, like a reporter barking out questions at a press conference.

He holds up the palm of his hand. "Whoa. I think I'm out of my depth here."

"She confided in you, right?"

"Can I plead the fifth, Madame Prosecutor?" he jokes, but then turns serious. "Summer, I don't think I'm in a position to…"

"What about my dad?" I say, my words tumbling over each other. "She said she was going to tell you some secret about my dad."

Mr. Kibbits' expression darkens.

I lean closer. "Tell me."

His jaw hardens. "Summer," he says firmly, "I don't share information my students tell me in confidence. Keep that in mind, if you ever need someone to confide in."

My eyes stay locked with his. "Shannon's dead," I remind him. "You can tell me."

He pats my arm. "You're a bright girl. As bright as your sister, I'm sure. If you're reading her journal, then I guess you're going to find out whatever was on her mind when she wrote it. But don't live in the past. For your own sake. Okay?"

I hold his gaze a moment longer, then sigh. I don't know whether I'm frustrated or relieved.

He smiles. "I'm here just about every Sunday at this time," he says. "And, of course, I'll be back in my classroom in the fall. If you need a sounding board, you'll know where to find me."

I nod, staring at my lap.

"If you need a sounding board about *anything*," he clarifies. "I'm sure your life is just as complicated as your sister's was at your age."

Except that Shannon's is frozen in time. Do I dare thaw it out?

Oh, God. Tell me I didn't just use ice as a metaphor.

———————

I grab an apple from a bowl in the kitchen after Gibs drops me off from the library.

Mom walks in with a basket of laundry as I take a bite. Even doing laundry on a Sunday afternoon, Mom looks ready for her close-up—slacks pressed, blouse crisp, makeup flawless. Her silvery-blond hair is pulled back into a chic ponytail.

"How was the library?" Mom asks. I didn't tell her why I was going, but her face had brightened at the mention of a library.

"It was okay. Hey, Mom?"

"Yes, dear?"

"You never did tell me why you stopped going to church."

She shifts the laundry basket from one hip to the other. "Goodness, Summer, what's up with all the questions today?"

I shrug. I'm still in intrepid-reporter mode. Mom's dodges and weaves aren't working today.

She grips the laundry basket tighter. An awkward moment hangs in the air. "So ... you *want* to go to church?" she asks again.

"No. I mean, I don't know. I don't *think* so."

I've really never thought much about it. We go to Mass with Grandma and Grandpa on Easter and Christmas, and Mom says "bless you" when someone sneezes and tells friends she's praying for them when they're going through hard times. That's about the extent of my exposure to religious life. I've never stopped to consider whether I wish it was different or if I have any strong feelings one way or the other.

"I just want to know why you stopped going," I tell Mom.

She puts the laundry basket on the kitchen table, plucks a hand towel from the top, and picks at it absently.

"I didn't understand why God took Shannon from me," she finally says in a small but steady voice. "I still don't. Didn't I do everything right? I *tried*."

I gasp a little. This is probably the most real thing Mom has ever said to me about Shannon. Has she just been waiting for me to ask?

I shrug, aiming for casual to avoid freaking Mom out. "Shannon's dying doesn't mean you did something wrong. Sometimes things just happen."

"Then what's the point of prayer?" Mom asks in a surprisingly sharp tone.

I shrug again and swallow hard.

"But that's not the main reason," Mom says, staring at

the towel. "Yes, I was mad at God—if there is a God. And I guess I still am. I never expected life to be perfect, but I didn't count on a blow like that. Losing a child...it's..."

She pauses, gripping the towel tighter.

"So, if there *is* a God, I'm pretty ticked off," she continues in a stronger voice. Her eyes search mine. "What do you think of people who question whether there is a God? I mean, if there really is a God, do you think he would condemn someone to eternal suffering just for having enough courage to admit that no one can know for sure?"

"Um..." Who am I kidding? I'm too stunned to speak. Mom is not only telling me real things, she's asking me real questions...seeking *my* opinion.

"I wouldn't want to worship that kind of a God," she says, not waiting for my answer. She loosens her grip on the hand towel and it falls back into the basket as she gazes into space. "Besides. Shannon was going through a...phase...when she died."

Her eyes flicker toward mine as if she's gauging my reaction. I don't move a muscle.

Mom peers past me. "I'd rather be in hell with my children than in heaven without them."

My throat tightens. I study her face as if I've never seen it before. She looks small and fragile. And sad. I want to reach out to her. Will she let me touch her?

But in the instant that I lean toward her, her eyes refocus, as if she's coming out of a trance. "Well," she says briskly, "better get my laundry done."

She reaches for her basket.

"Hey, Mom," I say abruptly.

"Yes?"

I pause. I don't really have anything to say. I just don't want her to go. So I ask, "Did you used to belong to a lot of clubs?"

Mom laughs at the sudden detour into more mundane territory. "Why would you ask that?"

I shift my weight. "Aunt Nic was mentioning some club you used to belong to. A book club, maybe?"

Confusion flickers in Mom's eyes, but then she nods. "Guilty as charged," she says. "I guess I was something of an extrovert when I was younger. I kind of outgrew that."

"Why?" I press. "Why would you stop doing things that you enjoyed?"

She looks annoyed. "Honestly, Summer, life's not about *enjoying* yourself all the time."

Whatever mood I'd caught Mom in five minutes earlier has officially passed. She's back.

My face flushes, and then Mom's eyes soften. She reaches out and gently squeezes my arm. "I didn't mean to snap," she says, then takes a deep breath. "Okay. Why did I quit joining things. Let's see. I got my realtor's license when you started kindergarten, and that's kept me plenty busy, as you know."

I nod. Her eyes stay locked with mine. She's not finished.

"You know," she says softly, "I used to think I had it all figured out. If I do *A*, then I can count on *B*. But you can't really count on anything. Control is just an illusion."

God. It *is* possible to have a conversation with my mother. Have I just never really tried before?

Mom looks in my eyes and smiles wearily. "I don't mean to bore you with my philosophizing, honey. Actually, I don't do much of *that* anymore, either. Kind of like the book club, I guess. Some things just . . . fade away."

She pats my arm, her fingers cool against my skin. Then she picks up her laundry basket. "Now, honey, please, I've got to get my laundry done."

"Okay." That's all I say.

I don't tell her what I'm thinking: *Sorry, Mom, but I don't believe you've changed as much as you think you have.*

Eleven

or you."

I glance up from my history book and see Gibs standing in front of me holding a dandelion.

"For good luck on your history test," he clarifies.

I smile, take the dandelion, blow the tendrils playfully in his face, then pat the space next to me on the picnic bench. He sits beside me.

"I'll miss jock patrol," I tell him wistfully.

I've long since blown off the cafeteria scene at school, preferring the solitude of the picnic table under a magnolia tree by the gym. I used to sit here alone reading a book during lunch, but Gibs has been joining me since we became friends. We observe sweaty athletes filing out of the gym in their basketball shorts and muscle shirts, or watch the drill team or cheerleaders practicing on the lawn, and feel infinitely above it all as we make corresponding snotty remarks.

Well, I should clarify. Gibs doesn't feel infinitely above anybody (he's the most humble guy I know), and he seldom makes snotty remarks. But he's a good enough sport to laugh at mine. Jock patrol is the highlight of my day, thanks to Gibs.

"I'll miss it, too," he says. "But I've already reserved this picnic bench for senior year. And we can hang out this summer, right?"

I fake-pout. "Mom's sentenced me to hard labor, remember?"

Gibs' eyes narrow.

"My aunt's flower shop," I remind him.

"Oh, right. How often do you work?"

I shrug. "I don't go back until Saturday. But after school is out, Aunt Nic will probably start giving me weekday hours. I'm sure we'll have time to hang out, though. Just you, me, and my raging allergies."

Leah Rollins and Kendall Popwell walk past the gym in shorts and cheerleading T-shirts, offering fluttery waves as they approach Gibs and me. Both girls' hair is flat-ironed into sleek, smooth submission—Leah's brown, Kendall's bottle-blond. Kendall is prettier but Leah is skinnier, and thinness trumps all in their circles. Besides, Leah's always the center of the universe, so Kendall just sort of orbits around her. I cringe, recalling my stint as Orbiter-in-Chief.

Gibs waves back gamely.

"How'd you do on the Chaucer test?" Leah asks him.

"Okay, I think," Gibs says.

Kendall snorts. "'Okay' probably means an A plus in Gibs' world," she says.

He's brushing off the compliment, explaining that Chaucer was really tough for him (yeah, right), but I'm not paying attention. A slow boil is simmering in my chest. I hate to sound petty, but it really chaps my ass that Leah and Kendall are reading Chaucer with Gibs in honors classes while the headiest reading they do in their spare time is *Cosmo*. I know, I know…I have no one to blame but myself for not being in those classes (I really could crack a textbook now and then, other than during finals). But honors courses should require thinking an original thought once or twice in your life, shouldn't they?

"Summer?" Leah says, and I realize she's repeating herself.

"Oh, sorry," I say. "What?"

"I asked what you're studying." She's inching closer, to peer at the history book I'm holding.

"History," I say.

"Yeah, but which one?"

Snothead. She loves rubbing my C-list academic standing in my face.

"Ms. Pilcher's class, right?" Kendall volunteers helpfully, making it clear that yes, that's the class one tier up from remedial.

"Right," I say evenly.

"Isn't Brice Casdorph in that class?" Kendall asks.

Touché. He's the one who was just arrested for vandalism.

"Mmmmmm," I reply.

"So your final is today?" Leah asks.

"Mmmmm."

"Well...good luck with that."

I manage a fake smile as they walk away. "Bitches," I murmur under my breath.

"What?" Gibs asks earnestly. "What did they say?"

I roll my eyes. "You don't get girl vibes at all, do you?"

He studies my face for a few seconds, then pulls a knee against his chest. "So," he says, changing the subject, "what's the latest with Shannon?"

Aaaahhh, Shannon. I'm tempted to tell him that I've been too busy with finals to think much about her, but the truth is, I'm nothing short of obsessed. *Did you kill yourself, Shannon? Please tell me you didn't kill yourself. I can't quite bear that thought. And what other secrets might you harbor? Anything that might, oh, I don't know, totally screw with my mind?*

Every morning on the way to school, I drive past the tree she hit—three blocks up the street from our house, a few yards past the stop sign after the right turn, past three ranch-style houses and around a little curve, right before a park just half a mile from the high school...

I've always known which tree it is (Mom and Grandma still place flowers there), but I never thought much about it until I started reading Shannon's journal. Now, that stupid giant oak tree practically taunts me, casting its gnarled branches like an arthritic Satan, looming over me like a gray, wizened wraith. It creeps me out to see kids playing near it on the swings and merry-go-round.

Thank God school will be over in a couple days and I won't have to drive past the tree again until senior year starts. But I can't avoid Shannon's journal. I haven't read any more of it since the night I opened it; finals actually feel like something of a godsend for once, an excuse to stay busy. But I can already feel her words luring me back, like the branches of that tree.

"Have you read any more of the journal?" Gibs asks.

"No," I say. "And maybe I won't."

He considers my words, then nods sharply.

But he knows. I can see in his eyes that he knows.

I'm not fooling anybody.

———

You'd figure I'd have big plans tonight, since I've just finished my last day of school. But you'd figure wrong. Gibs is at a Habitat for Humanity meeting (should I admit how much I miss him?) and I have to work at Aunt Nic's shop tomorrow, so I am actually calling it a night at the embarrassingly respectable hour of ten p.m. But not before I take a deep breath and reach for the journal I've tucked under my mattress. "Hi, Shannon," I say sleepily, then turn to her next entry.

Saturday, June 5, 1993

*I sneaked out last night to see Chris. I've perfected
my system: Dad checks the locks at ten o'clock every
night, then goes to bed. Mom stays up to watch
another hour of TV, then starts the dishwasher and
calls it a night.*

*The dishwasher is pretty quiet for the first ten
minutes or so, when it's filling up with water. But
then, the water starts churning and the motor sounds
like bullfrogs on speed. That's when I make my move,
slipping downstairs and out the sliding glass doors.
From that point, I walk across the deck and tiptoe
down the stairs into the back yard, Then all I have
to do is duck when I pass Mom's and Dad's bedroom
window, unlatch the gate, run down the side of the
yard, and walk a block down the street, where Chris
is waiting at the stop sign to pick me up.*

*Dad has caught me a couple of times sneaking
back in, but he just shakes his head. Who is Dad to
lecture me about sneaking around?*

*Chris and I are tossing around the M word.
Crazy, I know. I didn't even have my first date until
eleven months ago! While all my friends were flirting
and pairing up from, like, seventh grade on, I was
starting petitions to improve crosswalk signage. So
who knew I'd fall so hard and so fast for my first
real boyfriend? He wants to go into his dad's welding
business as soon as we graduate, so if I stay in town*

for college, we can get M'd right away. (I can't even bring myself to write down the word!) Chris says the M word stands for 'maybe later,' the stinker. But he's just kidding. Did I mention that Chris is the greatest guy in the free world? God, I love him so much.

In other news, Mom has blackmailed me into seeing a shrink. She said she'll take my car away if I don't. My first appointment is Monday. I think I'll mess with his mind by telling him I talk to trees and can make things spontaneously combust. No need to get into the messy truth that Mom is a control freak who thinks she can live my life.

She'll love the whole M plan. Maybe Chris and I will even live in a trailer. We'll have barbecues on Saturday nights and serve squirrel. She can wear her pearls.

I wonder if she bribed the shrink to install a computer chip in my head so she can program my life.

I shake my head slowly as I prop myself up on my elbow. Marriage? At seventeen? To a loser she had to sneak out of the house to see? No wonder Mom hired a shrink.

I know Mom's a control freak, Shannon, I think. *Nobody can relate to that better than I can. But, God, you're an idiot. No offense. And while I've got your attention ... would it kill you to spell out exactly what's up with Dad?*

Would it kill you. I've got to watch my figures of speech.

Twelve

Ah-choo.

I stab the stem of a crocus, pinning it into a foam wreath with gleeful intensity. Take *that,* you sneeze-maker.

Aunt Nic walks back to the work table and glances anxiously. "Oh, Summer, honey . . . all I need you to do is bring the flowers from the fridge to the work table. *I'll* do the arranging."

I laugh at her. "Don't worry, Aunt Nic, I wasn't going all *Better Homes and Garden* on you. I was just goofing around."

She smiles. "I'm sure you'll be helping me arrange flowers in no time. But it's only your second day."

I unpin the crocus from the wreath and toss it back into a pile with the others. "A girl can dream," I say.

What a place to spend my first official day of summer: Allergy Alley.

I don't really mind. I've always loved my Aunt Nic, and I guess there are worse things than hanging out with crocuses (croci?), even if they do assault my histamines.

Still, I can't get Shannon's journal off my mind. A thousand questions float through my head, and I wonder which ones Aunt Nic can answer. I decide to ask her the safest of them—which is still one of the questions Mr. Kibbits wouldn't answer.

"Did Shannon hate Mom?" I ask.

Aunt Nic picks up a crocus and fingers its satiny stem.

"No," she says in a small but firm voice. "She loved her."

I suck in my lips. "She's got a real hate-fest going on in her journal."

Aunt Nic smiles wryly. "I kind of got that gist from the first couple of pages. That's why I couldn't show it to your mother. It's why I couldn't keep reading." She eyes me warily. "How much have you read?"

I tuck a hand into my jeans pocket. "Just a few pages. I need to kind of … pace myself. This isn't the Shannon I was expecting."

Aunt Nic's eyes flood with remorse. "Oh, honey. Maybe I shouldn't have given it to you. I didn't mean to disillusion you."

I shake my head impatiently. "It's okay. It's real. It's who she was. What *is* it with our family, having to sanitize everything and make it all sparkly and antiseptic?"

Aunt Nic fingers her necklace. "Shannon was everything we told you she was—sweet and fun and loving and adorable, all of those things. She was just going through a rebellious phase. No matter what her journal says, please don't think that's the whole story. I changed that girl's *diapers,* Summer, just like I changed yours. I knew her. You have to believe me. She was an angel."

I grit my teeth and fling my hands in the air. "She wasn't an angel. Thank God I'm finally figuring that out."

Aunt Nic sighs. "Aren't all kids angels in their own families?"

I clench my fists. "No! *I'm* not."

She presses her palm against my cheek. "But you are! You are to *us.* That's what being in a family is all about."

I step back from her touch. "That's what being in *our* family is all about—being fake. That's what Shannon was rebelling against. That's why she hated Mom."

Aunt Nic thinks for a second, then crosses her arms. "Did you know that Grandma made your mother and me wear matching dresses until we were, like, twelve?"

I smile in spite of myself. "I've seen the pictures. Tragic."

Aunt Nic's eyes sparkle. "We rebelled around the time we were in middle school. But we loved it when we were kids. I don't have children, so I know I'm no authority, but … I think parents can be just what their kids need at some points in their lives, then *not* be what they need at other points."

She pauses for a moment, intertwining her fingers. "Yes, your mom is a perfectionist," she continues. "But frankly, so was Shannon. It worked great when Shannon was little. It was only when she got older that the perfectionism thing started driving her crazy. It was Shannon who changed, not your mother. Your mom couldn't quite keep up."

I shake my head. "If Shannon didn't mind Mom being a control freak when she was little, it's just because she was too young to know better. Mom should have let her be her own person."

Aunt Nic rubs the crocus stem again, looking wistful. "I don't know," she says softly. "I'm sorry Shannon was frustrated, but I kinda feel for your mom. Raising Shannon...it must have been like having a job that you do really well for years and years, then suddenly, with no warning, the rules change, and everything that used to work doesn't work anymore."

"But once Mom could see it wasn't working, why didn't she change?" I ask, my voice insistent. "She didn't even change for me."

Aunt Nic's jaw drops. "She completely changed for you! You've been a rebel since the day you were born. How could you have gotten away with that if your mother hadn't changed?"

I open my mouth to respond, then close it and shake my head in resignation. I don't think Aunt Nic gets the problem with Mom—that she always gives me so much to rebel *against*.

The door jingles as a customer walks into the flower shop. Aunt Nic smooths her shirt as she turns toward the front of the store.

"Hey, Aunt Nic?" I call.

She glances over her shoulder. "Yeah, honey?"

"If I have other questions, can I ask you?"

She smiles. "You can ask me anything."

My eyes follow her as she walks away. I wish Mom was as easy-going as Aunt Nic. God, I'd settle for her being as easy-going as Queen Elizabeth.

"Well, hi there!" I hear Aunt Nic chirp, up by the counter. "It's been forever since I've seen you, Leah!"

I raise an eyebrow. Oh, God. Leah.

I sigh and walk toward the front, too.

"Hi, Summer," Leah says with a stiff little smile. "You're working here?"

I nod. "How about you? What're you doing this summer?"

She shrugs. "Volunteer work, cheerleading camp. Oh, and Beta Club stuff. Hey, speaking of which, are you going to the conference in August?"

"I'm not *in* Beta Club," I remind her.

"Oh, right. Hey, how do you think you did on your finals?"

I dig my nails into my palms. "Okay."

She offers a fake smile. "*Great*! Good for you! Wasn't it sweet of Gibs to help you study?"

I wrinkle my nose.

"And if we're lucky," Leah says, "it kept him from studying too hard for *his* finals! I'm still in the running for valedictorian, but these honors classes—phew! I mean, I'm sure they're no tougher than your classes are to you ... I mean, everything's relative ..."

"Mmmmm. Say, are you still dating Justin?"

Leah's eyes fall, and I actually feel a little guilty. Word has already spread that Justin dumped her a couple days ago.

"No, we broke up," she says.

Aunt Nic smiles sympathetically. My muscles tighten a little. I'm hard-pressed to say I feel sorry for her—she certainly has never mustered any sympathy for *me*—but she does look awfully sad right now.

"Sorry," I say.

"Oh, boyfriends are a dime a dozen," Aunt Nic says cheerily. "You'll move on to the next guy and make him eat his heart out."

Leah blushes and smiles. "Well ... " she says, "are my mom's flowers ready?"

"Oh, right!" Aunt Nic walks toward a refrigerator and pulls out a gargantuan spray of pink and purple flowers. I eye the amaranthus and sneeze.

"Big party?" Nic asks absently as she rings up the order.

"My birthday party," Leah responds. "Mom goes a little overboard on everything. She invited, like, half the high school." She blushes suddenly as her faux pas registers, then offers me a nervous smile. I avert my gaze.

"Well ... thanks," Leah sputters, then grabs the vase. "Bye." I wave my fingers loosely as she walks out of the shop.

Aunt Nic crosses her arms and looks at me. "Not on the guest list?" she asks, wrinkling her nose.

"Go figure."

She looks at me closely. "What happened to you two? You used to be such good friends."

I shake my head. "Not really. Even when we were younger, she made sure I knew she was out of my league."

"No!" Aunt Nic protests. "You were wonderful friends!"

I smile and roll my eyes. "O-*kay*." I'm used to our family defining *wonderful* as how they want things to be. Whatever.

"Hope she has fun at her party," I say as I head toward the back of the shop, then mutter under my breath, "Maybe the amaranthus will make her break out in hives."

Thirteen

Whoosh.
Chugga, chugga, chugga.
Whoosh.
Chooga, chooga, chooga.

I pry my eyes open, squinting to adjust to the sunlight streaming through my blinds on this bright Sunday morning.

Mom's running the dishwasher. I groan. I'm used to it at night, but not in the morning. For some reason, it sounds as loud as a freight train at this hour. What better way to start off one of the few mornings I can actually sleep in?

I spend a couple of minutes trying to get back to sleep, but it's impossible. I roll my eyes and prop my pillow against my headboard. Gibs and I are meeting for burgers later, but I've got time to kill for now, so...

I reach under my mattress for Shannon's journal. I press my lips together as my stomach muscles tighten, then open it to her next entry.

Monday, June 7, 1993

Confession: The shrink isn't nearly as hideous as I expected.

I thought he'd start our "session" by asking, "How does that make you feel?" any time I told him anything. But instead he told me he was a Deadhead, then talked about all the concerts he's been to. He showed me a picture on his desk of him with Jerry Garcia. He's been to lots of Stones concerts, too, and Bob Dylan. I told him he was living in the sixties and he laughed.

Then Dr. Deadhead asked me what kind of music I like, and I said, "I don't know."

He said, "How can you not know?"

Touché.

If he'd asked me a year earlier what kind of music I like, I would've told him the Grateful Dead, the Rolling Stones, and Bob Dylan. Because that's what HE likes, and that's how desperate I always was to please. I have no personality. I'm not a real person. I'm just a blank slate. Write on me however you see fit, and I'll find a way to be that person. All I ask in return is that you like me.

How pathetic.

So I've stopped trying to be a blank slate. I just don't know what to be instead. I spent so long guessing how other people want me to be, then playing that part, that I don't know how to BE. I just know how to ACT.

So the simplest question in the world—"what kind of music do you like?"—made me cry.

Because the answer scares the hell out of me: I have no idea.

———

"She was seeing a psychologist."

Gibs raises an eyebrow as he drinks from a straw.

I dab a French fry into the catsup I've squirted onto my burger wrapper.

"A shrink," I clarify. Gibs has this habit of not responding right away, and it always makes me feel like I have more explaining to do.

"I know what a psychologist is," he says, setting his soft drink back on the table.

Little kids with catsup-smeared T-shirts run past us squealing, headed for the adjoining play area and leaving a harried-looking mom in their wake.

"She talks about the shrink in her journal?" Gibs asks, taking a bite of his burger.

I nod, my eyes still fixed on the kids as they dive head-first into a vat of brightly colored balls. "She says Mom threatened to take her car away if she didn't go."

She says. Present tense. I'm referring to Shannon in the present tense.

"Does she say why your mom wanted her to see a shrink?" Gibs asks.

My eyes finally pull away from the kids and settle back onto Gibs' face. "She's acting weird all of a sudden," I tell him. "Shannon's been a goody-goody all her life, and now she's feeling phony and suffocated. She can't even tell the shrink what kind of music she likes. She says that now that she's stopped playing the goody-goody role, she doesn't know who she is."

Gibs shrugs. "Everybody plays a role," he says quietly. "My cousin's in medical school because when she was in kindergarten, some relative asked her what she wanted to be when she grew up. She said a doctor. You know, like some kids say they want to be a pirate. Anyway, from that point on, her parents bragged to anybody who would listen that she was going to medical school."

I crinkle my brow. "So you're saying she doesn't really want to be in medical school?"

"Who knows? But that's a lot of pressure, you know?"

"So nobody does what they really want to do? They're all just trying to please somebody?"

"Or *displease* somebody. Like you. By being a screw-up in school."

My eyes narrow mischievously. "Has it ever occurred to you that I'm just not very bright?"

He considers my question for a moment, then says, "Leah Rollins is a straight-A student. She takes notes when a teacher mentions he got his tires rotated over the weekend. Asks if it's going to be on the test." Gibs sips his drink. "But she's learned how to play the game. She might even end up valedictorian. Not that I'm bitter. My point is that grades have a minimal correlation to intelligence."

"You're a straight-A student, too," I remind him.

He nods. "Yet I have much more in common with you than I do with Leah Rollins."

He glances past me and his eyes widen slightly. "Speak of the devil…"

I turn around and see Leah and Kendall Popwell coming through the door, their sleek, straight hair flowing. I roll my eyes and slink lower in my seat.

Gibs waves in their direction. Damn. They've spotted us. They walk over to our table.

"Hi, Gibson. Hi, Summer," Leah says.

I toss a noncommittal wave.

"What's up?" Gibs asks.

"Just grabbing lunch," Kendall responds.

"Are you doing extra IB work this summer?" Leah asks Gibs.

"Uh, yeah. My advisor recommended it," Gibs says.

I roll my eyes. IB, or the International Baccalaureate Program, is our school's most elite honors program, intended for either the freakishly brilliant (think Gibs) or the most freakishly slavish to school conformity (think Leah).

"Just be sure to come up for air every once in a while,"

Leah tells Gibs with a smile. "You're edging me out for class valedictorian, you know. My mom is *not* pleased."

Gibs blushes.

"You're *both* edging me out," Kendall says in mock indignation. "Slack up a little, will ya?"

"Check," Gibs says, smiling shyly.

"Well, better be going," Leah says. "See ya." The girls walk toward the counter to order their meals.

I narrow my eyes. "*See ya*," I repeat, in a breathy Leah imitation.

Gibs laughs. "Leah's nice enough," he says.

"Leah's a snake," I correct him. Why do guys never get these things?

"Anyway, back to Shannon," I say impatiently, tapping a French fry against my burger wrapper. "I wonder if Shannon's psychologist is still around. She hasn't called him by name, at least not so far. She calls him Dr. Deadhead."

"Even if he *is* still around, he wouldn't be able to talk about Shannon," Gibs says. "Doctors can't discuss their patients."

"Shannon's dead," I remind him.

"Doesn't matter. My parents are doctors. Patient confidentiality is sacrosanct."

"Ooooh," I tease, tossing another fry into my mouth. "I bow to your superior intellect. After all, your parents are *doctors*."

He smiles, blushes, and stares at the table. "I didn't mean it like that."

"You totally did. You are such a show-off."

Gibs squeezes his eyes shut and shakes his head, his cheeks still rosy.

"I'm kidding, moron," I tell him. "You're the *anti*-show-off."

He sips from his drink, still too embarrassed to look at me.

"I thought we were talking about Shannon," he finally says after taking a swallow.

I giggle. "Can you handle even the slightest amount of attention?"

He drums his fingers on the table. "Feeling a little self-conscious here, Summer."

"Yeah, duh." I study him carefully, resting my chin on the palm of my hand. "You're quite the dichotomy, Gibson Brown. You manage to stand out in a million different ways, what with your freakish intelligence and all, yet you can't handle the most casual conversation about yourself."

"Oh, I can handle it," he says playfully, finally sneaking a glance at me.

"Can you really? Let's see about that. Okay, Gibs, tell me what you consider to be your best quality."

He grins sheepishly. God, he's got the cutest dimple. "I'm unbelievably patient with inane questions," he says.

"And your worst?"

He thinks for a second. "Even though I humor my friends when they're asking me inane questions, I'm secretly plotting revenge."

I lean closer. "Intriguing. And what shape might this revenge take?"

He waves an arm nonchalantly through the air. "Something like this." He squeezes a half-empty catsup packet in my direction and it spews in my face.

I sputter with laughter. "Oh, *no you didn't!*" I shake pepper into my hand and blow it toward his face.

He fans his face as I dab the catsup off my cheek. People start looking at us as we laugh.

"You're making a spectacle of yourself," I say, feigning indignation.

"Yeah, you tend to bring that out in me." He grins, relaxing into his booth.

God, that *dimple*.

Fourteen

Friday, June 11, 1993
Jamie Williams, meet Journal.

The handwriting changes from Shannon's fat, bouncy letters to a messy, slanted scrawl:

Hi, Journal.

Back to Shannon:

Jamie's spending the night with me. Grandma and Grandpa ate dinner with us tonight, so she got the whole Twenty Questions routine while she was trying to pick the onions out of her meatloaf. In keeping with the question/answer theme, I'll quiz Jamie now.

Q. How did you like my mother's meatloaf?

A. The onions grossed me out. I think your mom noticed. Just one more reason for her to hate me, I guess.

Q. Haven't you learned yet how to suck up to my mom?

A. I'm trying. She shot me a dirty look when I walked into the dining room wearing a tube top, and the new piercing on the top of my earlobe didn't win me any brownie points. Also, I got seriously bad vibes when your grandparents asked me what I was doing after graduation and I said chilling. Can't your mother take a joke?

Q. Except that you weren't joking.

A. Whatever.

Q. Speaking of bad vibes, do you still hate Chris?

A. For the zillionth time: I DO NOT HATE CHRIS!!! I just don't think he's good enough for you. Gawd. I wish I'd never told you about Tiffany.

Q. He already told me about Tiffany. He wasn't flirting with her at the party. He was helping her find her contact lens. For the zillionth time: GET YOUR MIND OUT OF THE GUTTER!!!!

A. That's not a question.

Q. Okay, here's the question: Do you finally accept that Chris was only helping Tiffany find her contact lens at the party?

A. Assuming her contact lens fell into her shirt and that they had to turn off the lights to look for it. New subject pleeze!

Q. Are you sure you're not just jealous that for the first time ever, I've got a boyfriend and you don't?

A. You've always loved awards, so tonight I'm pleased to present you with the trophy for Most Conseated.

Q. "Conceited." And no, I'm not. I just want my best friend to be happy for me that I finally know what it's like to be in love. Oh, sorry. That's not a question. How's this: Can you be happy for me that I finally know what it's like to be in love?

A. As soon as I finish barfing, I'll start being happy for you.

Q. Will you be the maid of honor at my wedding?

A. As long as you don't ask Tiffany to be a bridesmaid. Or at least insist she wear her glasses at the wedding. We wouldn't want any contact lens snafus during the ceremony, now would we? And speaking of weddings, does your mom know yet that you're thinking of trading Harvard for buy-one-get-one-free tuition at Moron Community College?

Q. I'm asking the questions here. And Morton is a perfectly good college.

A. Perfectly good if you want to file nails for a living. And by the way, you're totally not getting the whole Q-and-A concept.

Q. Here's a question: Ready to ditch the journal?

A. Gawd yes. I haven't done this much writing since my second year of freshman English. And I'm dying to smoke some weed, so get the air freshener ready. Bye, journal.

I listen to crickets chirp outside my window and squeeze the cover of the journal. I have to get up early tomorrow morning for work, but even though my eyes are heavy, I can't put the journal aside.

Eighteen years earlier, Shannon's friend Jamie was sleeping in *my* house, just down the hall. They'd had dinner earlier that evening in *my* dining room, with *my* parents and grandparents, and then they'd gone upstairs and started writing in the journal I'm holding now. And smoking weed! All this time, I'd thought *I* was the rebel in the family. I can't help feeling exasperated. *I'm rebellious, Shannon, but not stupid. Why are you such a follower? Could your little phase possibly be any more clichéd?*

But I take a deep breath as I remember the entry that has haunted me since I first opened the journal: *I want to kill myself.* Beneath all her breezy bravado, Shannon was really hurting.

I keep reading:

Saturday, June 12, 1993

Okay, so I kinda admit the whole Chris-helping-Tiffany-find-her-contact-lens deal was bugging me more than I wanted to admit, so I told him to meet me at the park tonight. I told my probation officer (AKA Mom) that I needed to make a drugstore run to buy tampons, so that bought me a little time away from the Big House.

I got to the park, took one look at Chris sitting on a tire swing in the moonlight, and burst into tears. Corny, I know. What can I say? He has that effect on me.

I bawled my eyes out while I told him that I totally trust him but keep hearing rumors about him and Tiffany and just don't know what to think. He held me for the longest time … just the two of us sitting on the swing in an empty park.

What he told me makes perfect sense. First, consider the source. Yes, I've heard the rumors from several people, but most of those people heard the rumors from Jamie, and Chris is right: Jamie is totally jealous of me. She's a great friend, but I don't think she can accept my relationship with Chris, especially since she's boyfriendless at the moment. It's a total role reversal for us, and I just don't think she can handle it. So I don't (entirely) blame her for stirring up gossip, but I can't let her jealousy mess up the best thing that's ever happened to me.

So what have I learned?

- Trust Chris. He would never hurt me. We're going to spend the rest of our lives together, *proving our love. Repeat after me: CHRIS IS NOT MY DAD.*

- *Don't trust Jamie. Not entirely, anyway.*
- *Necking on a squeaky, rusty tire swing under the stars is the most romantic thing in the world.*

Note to self: If your excuse for getting out of the house is that you're making an emergency tampon run, don't come home empty-handed.

You guessed it: My hall monitor (AKA Mom) was waiting for me at the front door when I came home from the park. She had that George Washington expression on her face, the cold eyes and the lips stretched into a tight straight line. I played it cool and told her I realized I was low on gas when I got in the car, so I spent my last ten bucks on petro instead of tampons.

So what was I going to do without tampons, she asked.

Well, it just so happens I ran into Eve at the gas station and she lent me a few spares she had in her purse.

Would I care to produce them, Mom asked.

Thank God I had a couple of tampons in the bottom of my bag.

Except that then, Mom produced the two full boxes of tampons she'd found under the bathroom sink.

Must have overlooked them, I said.

Except that we always keep them in the same place, so how could I have overlooked them, Mom asked.

Because OMIGOD, MOM, YOU'RE ALWAYS ON MY CASE! CAN'T I HAVE ONE SECOND OF PEACE WITHOUT BEING TREATED LIKE A SERIAL KILLER ON DEATH ROW?

Or something to that effect. I expected Mom to keep arguing, or keep lecturing, or start wailing about how my life was going to hell in a handbasket, but she didn't do any of those things. She just looked sad and went back to bed.

Which means I got off easy, right?

So why am I crying?

God, Mom can still push all my guilt buttons. Why? Wasn't 17.5 years of perfection enough for her? Aren't I entitled to tell an occasional lie? Okay, so they aren't so occasional these days, but maybe I'm making up for lost time. It seems the more right I did everything, the more Mom criticized me and kept upping the ante: "An A on your report card? But you made an A-plus last semester! What in God's name is wrong with you?!?" Or: "First runner-up in Miss Corncob USA? Oh, the horrors! We'll start training IMMEDIATELY for the next pageant! Snap to it, Shannon! Nothing but absolute perfection will ever be good enough for me!"

But I'M feeling guilty now? Mom never once

said to me, "Gosh, honey, I've been awfully hard on you, and I just want you to know: trophies or no trophies, honors or no honors, I think you're great just the way you are."

Truly, I'd give my right arm to hear that.

But I'll never hear it. Maybe Mom's the one who should feel guilty.

I close the journal, squeeze it under my mattress, lie on my side and stare into space. My head is spinning from all the information Shannon has thrown at me. I wish she'd learned what I learned early on—there's no pleasing Mom, so just take yourself out of the game. No beauty pageant equals no disappointment.

But then I wince a little. God knows I was never cut out to be a beauty queen, but maybe *some* of the games I took myself out of were things I might actually have enjoyed... might actually have been good at. Who had the right idea? Shannon, for tap-dancing for Mom as long and as hard as she could, or me, for refusing to put on the tap shoes in the first place?

As jolting as these thoughts are, my brain keeps going back to something else she wrote:

Repeat after me: CHRIS IS NOT MY DAD.

I pull the covers tighter under my chin. I can't quite wrap my head around it, but I can't wish it away, either.

So who was she, Dad? Who was the other woman?

Although I don't think I want to know, I'm starting to realize I don't have any choice. Shannon wants to tell me.

Fifteen

"id my dad have an affair?"

I'd planned on easing into the conversation, but it isn't working out that way.

Aunt Nicole's face turns pale. Here she is, innocently opening the door of her flower shop on a sunny Monday morning, her crisp white smock tied with a bow at her waist, and I'm asking her about my dad's affair before she can say hello.

"Well, good morning to you, too, Summer." She takes a deep breath, holds the door open and waves me inside.

"Sorry," I tell her. "I didn't mean to freak you out. I just…I don't know…I just need to know, and I can't exactly ask my parents."

Aunt Nicole flips the *CLOSED* sign to *OPEN* and shuts the door. The bell jingles.

She cocks her head toward the back of the store, and I follow her to the plaid loveseat in the workroom.

"Sit," she says. She chews on her bottom lip as we settle onto the sofa.

"I *knew* I shouldn't have given you that journal," she says wearily, tossing her head back and staring at the ceiling.

"It's true. He did have an affair." I say it matter-of-factly, knowing for sure now. It almost feels like a relief, like getting a diagnosis that confirms an awful disease but gives you the satisfaction of totally explaining your symptoms.

"I am *not* having this conversation with you," Aunt Nicole moans, covering her face with her hands.

"Was it just a fling? Or was it really serious? How long did it last? Did Mom find out? And just one affair, right?" Oh, God. Maybe not.

Aunt Nicole rubs the bridge of her nose, her eyes squeezed shut. "Here's the thing," she says. "You don't need to know this. You *shouldn't* know this. Kids aren't supposed to know everything about their parents. Truly, Summer, if I had any idea Shannon wrote about that, I never would have…" She opens her eyes and looks at me warily. "But I'd rather you have the big picture than some out-of-focus little snapshot." Then she turns wistful. "That Shannon," she says dreamily. "Keeping us on our toes even now."

"The affair," I prod her.

Aunt Nicole opens her mouth to speak, shuts it, opens it again, then says, "Your father is a good man."

"Proceed," I say dryly.

"It's funny," she says, touching her chin with her index finger. "Your parents are so different—your mom so assertive and opinionated, your dad so quiet. Some people thought they were too different to make a good match, but I always thought he was good for her. He calmed her down."

I make a rolling motion with my hand.

"Right. Anyway, your dad...he's the kind of person everybody assumes is content because he never says much." Her eyes suddenly lock with mine. "And I'm sure he *is* content, most of the time. He's a simple guy. As long as his family is happy, he's happy."

"Especially when he's having an affair," I observe, wishing my flat tone could quell the turbulence in the pit of my stomach.

Aunt Nicole shakes her head. "It wasn't like that. He's not the kind of man to have affairs. She threw herself at him."

I swallow hard. "She."

Aunt Nicole blushes and rubs her hands together. "She was the church secretary. Your parents went to church back then. We all went to Mass together on Sundays—Uncle Matt and me, your family, Grandma and Grandpa—then we'd alternate houses for a potluck lunch.

"Anyway, your dad would go back to the church after lunch so he could count the collection money. He did that for years, no big deal, until this *twit* moved into town and got a job as the church secretary."

"Who was she?" I ask, leaning closer.

Aunt Nicole waves away the question, as if the woman's identity is no more consequential than the amount of money in the collection basket. "I honestly don't even remember her name. Donna, maybe? Dana? Whatever. It only lasted a couple of months, then she disappeared as quickly as she'd blown into town."

"How did Shannon find out?'" I ask.

Aunt Nicole's hand fumbles across her mouth. She stares at her lap. "She walked in on them, honey."

I suck in a breath.

"They were just kissing," Aunt Nicole adds quickly. "That might have been all they ever did. But Shannon was devastated. We were still finishing up dessert at my house and your mom realized your dad had forgotten his glasses, so Shannon brought them to him at the rectory. She came back to my house half an hour later, white as a sheet."

"Did she tell Mom?" I ask, my voice quavering now.

Aunt Nicole shakes her head. "No. She didn't say anything for days, not even to me. But it was just a matter of time before the whole church was talking about it. The rectory was locked when Shannon got there, and some lady on the landscaping committee was planting azaleas and let her in with her key. The two of them, Shannon and the azalea lady, walked in together, and ..."

Both of us stare at our hands. I hate Dad right now.

"The azalea lady spread the word pretty quickly, and within a couple of weeks, it filtered down to your mother," Aunt Nicole says. "Shannon had already told me by then.

She realized the gossip was heating up and wanted to know how she could protect your mom."

"I thought that parents were supposed to protect their kids," I mutter.

Aunt Nicole's eyes flood with sadness. "I know, honey. It was awful."

I sigh. "I already know how this story ends."

Her eyebrows crinkle. "What do you mean?"

"I know my parents. I know *Mom*. I'm guessing that even while the whole church was gossiping about it, she was busy arranging the next yard sale and pretending it never happened. She probably called Dad at work the day she found out and reminded him to pick up a gallon of milk on his way home."

Aunt Nic holds a hand loosely over her mouth to cover a subtle smile.

"What?" I demand.

She considers her words for a second, then says, "You really don't know your mom as well as you think you do."

I lean in.

"The *first* thing she did," Aunt Nic says, "was kick your dad out of the house."

I gasp a little, mostly because I can't imagine Dad without Mom. Sure, they can go whole days without uttering more than a sentence to each other, but they're kind of symbiotic. I know Mom could do okay on her own, but Dad? He'd be like a plant without oxygen.

"Where did he go?" I ask.

Nic peers into space, trying to retrieve the memory in

her head. "Your Uncle Phil's, maybe? He started out in a motel, but that just lasted a few days. Then he moved in with his brother."

"In *Charlotte*?" I ask. "Two hours away?"

She nods. "He commuted to work every day. He told your mom he didn't want to waste any more money on a motel, that he wanted every spare cent of his paycheck to go to her and Shannon. He was so ashamed."

"I can't imagine Dad without Mom," I say.

Aunt Nic nods. "He was really pitiful. As mad as we all were at him, we couldn't help feeling sorry for him. He was just... lost without his family."

I absently pick up a flower from the work table and finger a satiny petal. "So when did he move back in?" I ask.

Aunt Nic thinks some more. "After about a month. I'm pretty sure... I don't think your mom had really planned to kick him out for good. She just wanted to teach him a lesson." Her eyes skitter away. "God, she was so upset that he put Shannon through that."

I swallow hard. Poor Shannon. No wonder she went off the deep end that summer. She must have been so confused, wondering if her whole life was one big fraud. Here she'd been expected to be perfect, but the people she'd trusted the most were nothing but phonies.

My eyes lock with Aunt Nic's again. "Did Mom ever confront the slut?"

She laughs nervously. "Uh, yeah."

"What happened?" I persist.

Nic shifts her weight and crosses her arms. "Your mom

was going to confront her at church, but the priest convinced her not to. He said she'd turned in her resignation and was leaving town, and that your mom should just leave well enough alone, that she was too classy to stoop to that level anyhow."

"But...?" I prod.

Aunt Nic's eyes sparkle. "But your mom and I ran into her in the grocery store. I saw her first. I tried to distract your mom by pulling her into another aisle, but she caught a glimpse of that frizzy orangy perm out of the corner of her eye. And then—standing ramrod straight and acting cool as a cucumber—your mother picked up an orange and walked over to the ... well, okay, the slut. I got close enough to overhear her threatening to affix that orange in a certain orifice if she ever messed with your family again."

She giggles, but I'm too stunned to giggle back. "God, this is tacky," I moan.

Aunt Nic nods, still laughing lightly. "You don't mess with Susanne's family," she says, then looks at me closer. "That goes for you, too, you know. There's nothing she wouldn't do for you, nobody she wouldn't protect you from."

I narrow my eyes. "So, my whole she-swept-it-under-the-rug theory...?"

Nic smiles and tousles a lock of my hair. "Yeah, that was a bit of a miscalculation, honey."

I smile back, plucking the petal off the rose. "I kinda like this side of Mom."

Sixteen

ad's in the den checking golf scores on the computer when I get home from the flower shop that afternoon. A baseball game on TV drones in the background.

"Hi, hon," he says, without turning around.

I study the back of his head, flecks of gray blended into golden-brown hair. He still has most of his hair, but it's thinning. Otherwise, he still looks like what I always imagined a superhero would look like under the mask.

He *seemed* like a superhero. I remember riding in the front seat of the car when I was little and the passenger door suddenly flying open while Dad was going sixty miles per hour on the interstate. I didn't even have time to scream before Dad had swung his long arm over my chest, grabbed the handle with the tips of his fingers and pulled it shut. He never took his eyes off the road. He didn't say anything about it—we just kept driving—but I felt safe. Dad's heroism was so effortless that it didn't even require commentary.

Although Dad and I have never had any heart-to-hearts, he's the one to toss me a sympathy glance when Mom starts nagging. He also likes to put little surprises—a pack of gum, a tube of lip gloss—in weird places where he knows I'll eventually find them, like in one of my socks. I walked around all day in school once wondering why my sweatshirt felt like it was choking me before I realized Dad had put an apple in the hood when he was kissing me goodbye that morning. He never talks about the quirky stuff he does; he just does it, then gets a twinkly look in his eyes when he knows that I've noticed.

I plop into the recliner, swiveling in Dad's direction. His eyes stay glued on the computer screen for another moment or two, but I guess it's pretty hard to concentrate when someone is staring at the back of your head, so he slowly turns to face me.

"Hi," I say.

His hand bobs in the air. "Hi."

"Can you tell me something?" I ask.

"Sure."

"Tell me something about Shannon."

His green eyes crinkle. "Something about Shannon..."

"Right. Something I don't already know."

To my astonishment, he doesn't stall. Instead, he peers

skyward, taps his chin, and says, "Hmmmm...something you don't already know..."

"Right," I say.

He smiles. "I used to call her Kerfluffle."

I smile to mask a stab of envy. Dad's never had a nickname for me.

"Where did that come from?" I ask, trying to sound breezy.

He shakes his head, still smiling. "Who knows. I remember I lost her in the park once—well, I *thought* she was lost, but actually she was hiding—and I was dashing around calling, 'Shannon! Shannon!' Finally, I called, 'Kerfluffle!' and she popped her head out from behind a tree and said, 'That's the name I was waiting to hear!'" We laugh lightly.

"She used to make me play Barbies with her," Dad continues, his eyes soft. "She'd have some dialogue worked out in her head, and she'd get frustrated when I didn't follow the script. She'd say, 'Where do you want to go today, Ken?' and I'd say, 'The movies?' She'd whisper, 'The mall.' Like we couldn't have Barbie and Ken overhearing the stage directions. So I'd say, 'The mall sounds good.'"

My smile is genuine now. Dad looks ten years younger.

"Did you and Shannon ever go to the mall together?" I ask.

He wrinkles his nose. "I wasn't much for shopping. That was something she and Mom would do together, like you and Mom do...well, like you and Mom *would* do, if you liked shopping. I guess you take after me, that way."

I lean closer and settle my chin on my hand. "How did Shannon take after you?"

He peers past me. "In no way whatsoever. She was everything I wasn't: bubbly, extroverted, witty, talented..." He clears his throat. "Of course, you're all those things, too," he says.

My back arches and I fold my arms across my chest. "You don't have to say that." I sound icier than I'd intended. Oh God. I sound like Mom.

Dad stares at his fingers. *Dammit.* I actually had him talking and now he's shutting down.

"Chinese, anyone?"

Dad and I look up, alarmed. Mom has just breezed into the room without us noticing.

"I picked up moo goo gai pan on my way home from work," she says, rifling through the mail. "It's in the kitchen."

Dad looks at me apologetically. He knows I want him to keep talking, but he's so damned relieved he doesn't have to.

Mom looks up from the mail to survey my jeans and T-shirt. "You went to work dressed that way?" she asks, curling her lip.

"She looks fine," Dad says, surprising both Mom and me.

Mom raises an eyebrow at him, then turns her attention back to me. "I talked to Ms. Beacham today."

"Mmmmmm."

"Your counselor," Mom qualifies.

I don't say anything, but I guess my expression says duh, because Mom turns snappish.

"Don't have that attitude with me, young lady."

I contain the urge to roll my eyes as she pauses to let the words sink in.

"*Anyway,*" she finally continues, "I called her because your SAT scores were in my email this morning."

I furrow my brow. "*Your* email?"

"Yes, my email, Summer. It's *my* test, after all. *I* paid for it."

"Well, how did you do?"

Even Dad chuckles slightly at that one, but Mom's withering glance stops him cold.

"Actually, you did quite wonderfully," Mom says, but her tone is accusatory. "You scored in the seventieth percentile nationwide in math, which you're always claiming is your worst subject. And the ninety-fourth percentile nationwide on the verbal section. The ninety-fourth percentile, Summer!"

Dad and I exchange confused glances.

"That's good, right?" I ask cautiously.

"Yes, it's good!" Mom snaps.

Okay, now I'm seriously confused.

"It's better than good, Summer. It's exceptional. You're exceptionally smart. Do you get that?"

Oh. I'm starting to get it.

"So there are no excuses whatsoever for a young lady who scores in the ninety-fourth percentile nationwide to be squeaking by in school with barely a C average!"

Dad taps the computer keyboard idly. "Let's not talk about Summer's grades right now," he says quietly. "Let's just enjoy how well she did on the SATs."

"I will never understand," Mom continues, her voice fairly booming, "how mediocrity became an acceptable standard for you, Summer!"

"Susanne..." Dad says softly.

"Because it's not acceptable to me! It's not acceptable to your father! It certainly won't be acceptable to the colleges you're applying to next fall! Do you get that, Summer? Do you get how you're narrowing your options? How you have the intelligence to go to an Ivy League school, yet your laziness is dooming you to... to... I shudder to think what schools would accept you with your GPA. Perhaps *Morton Community College*?"

Even amid my irritation at Mom's tirade, the irony is not lost on me. The summer before her senior year, Shannon was crossing Harvard *out* of her future and penciling Morton Community College *in* so that she could stay close to Chris. God. If Mom only knew.

"And with all of your potential..."

As Mom rambles on, I realize that Dad is sidling inconspicuously out of his seat and heading toward the kitchen. It's dinner time.

Mom doesn't notice. She's still yammering.

I think about the church secretary. I hate Dad for having an affair, but I can't help wondering how good it must have felt for him to stop feeling invisible for a while.

Seventeen

Sunday, June 13, 1993
Eve called me tonight after dinner. She said
my mom had called her mom to tell her she was so
glad we ran into each other at the gas station last
night. Except that Eve was home all night watching
a movie with her mom and sister.

Eve said she was sorry she'd blown my alibi,
but I told her it was okay. Mom hadn't believed me
anyway. Then Eve wanted to know why I'd needed
an excuse in the first place, and she got really quiet
when I told her I'd met Chris at the park.

I felt like screaming, "Please stop judging me,
Evie!"

Our friendship has been pretty much over since
Spring Fling. Eve was stunned—STUNNED!—

that Chris invited me. "You two have nothing in common!" she told me. Like it made no sense that someone as cute and cool as Chris could ever possibly be interested in me. Thanks, "friend."

Eve didn't get invited, so I asked her to come over and help me with my hair and nails before Chris picked me up. I wasn't trying to rub it in that she didn't have a date. I thought it would make her feel included. Anyway… she dissed me, and things have been awkward ever since. I started sitting with Jamie in the lunchroom while Eve sat at our old table reading a book. I keep telling myself it's no biggie. Just because someone's been your best friend for umpteen years doesn't mean she needs to be your best friend the rest of your life, especially if she can't even be happy for you during the most exciting time in your life. And Jamie's so much fun! She never makes me feel judged.

Still…

I don't know. It just felt really good to hear Eve's voice when she called.

I set the journal aside, pick up the cell phone from my bedside table, and call Gibs.

"I know my dad's secret," I say, as soon as he answers.

He pauses.

"Yeah," I say wearily. "It's what you think it is. God. Men are so predictable."

Gibs is still silent.

"An affair," I clarify.

"Oh," he says. "I'm sorry."

"Shannon walked in on them. He was having some fling with the church secretary—God, how tacky is that?—and Shannon caught them kissing in the rectory."

"Bummer," Gibs says softly. "But...you sound okay. *Are* you okay?"

My eyes unexpectedly fill with tears, but I blink them back. "Yeah. Whatever."

"That must have really done a number on Shannon," Gibs says.

I nod. "I think it messed with her mind. I know everybody thought she had it all together, Gibs, but she was really naïve. You can read it in her words. It's like she lived in a bubble, and when Dad popped it, she went from one extreme to the other—Miss Priss to Bad Ass in one fell swoop. But it was just an act. She was so sad and confused." *I want to kill myself...*

"It makes me so mad at Mom," I add.

"At your mom?" Gibs says. "Why your mom?"

"I don't know...At first, with the affair, I sympathized with her, especially after Aunt Nic told me how she went all ninja on the other woman when she saw her in the grocery store."

"What?"

"Something about shoving an orange up her ass. Anyway, she was like this total mother bear, you know, ready to practically claw somebody's eyes out to protect her family. So *that* was kinda cool. But..."

"But what?"

I shrug. "She treats Dad like dryer lint. She's totally bossy and bitchy. She never pays any attention to him."

"Maybe she paid him plenty of attention until he cheated on her," Gibs observes.

I open my mouth to respond, but nothing comes out.

"So do your parents know you know?" Gibs asks.

I crinkle my nose. "*What?*"

"Your parents. Do they know you know about your dad's affair?"

I laugh out loud. "God, no!"

"Why would it be so weird for them to know? I mean, they know Shannon knew, right?"

"That doesn't mean anybody ever *talked* about it," I say. "Shannon said it herself in the journal—my parents never talk about anything that matters."

"But *you're* the one not talking about it," Gibs says.

I cluck my tongue impatiently. "Could *you* talk to your parents about something like this?"

"I don't know," Gibs muses. "I know my dad got a girl pregnant in medical school. We talk about that."

I gasp. "Really? What happened to the girl?"

Gibs laughs. "She became my mother. I was the baby."

I smile in spite of myself. I've only met Gibs' parents in passing, but who would have guessed. "Still," I say, "that turned out okay."

"But your dad's affair turned out okay, too. I mean, your folks are still married."

Which makes sense, right? They *are* still married.

Only that doesn't strike me as a success.

Eighteen

Monday, June 14, 1993

When I met with Dr. Deadhead last Monday, I gave him an earful about how Mom's a control freak and Dad's a hypocrite, but he didn't want to talk about those things today. (And I have so much more to say!)

He asked me about my friends. I told him how Eve and I have drifted apart and how Jamie and I have gotten so close. He did that sneaky shrink thing of getting information without asking many questions, and the next thing I knew, I was telling him things that made him take lots of notes.

I know he's thinking the same thing Mom thinks: Eve is Miss Perfect, Jamie is Trouble, blah, blah, blah, blah, blah. I HATE the way adults put people in tiny boxes: good, bad, smart, stupid, right, wrong. I spent most of my life believing them. Then I gave Miss Wrong a chance and found out she's really fun. And Miss Right started to seem pretty judgmental.

So, Dr. Deadhead, why am I wrong for giving people the benefit of the doubt?

He said he didn't think I was wrong, just maybe a little naïve.

But naïve is what I USED to be. I was naïve when I thought Mom could never be wrong, that Dad could never make a mistake. Dr. Deadhead asked if I could say these things to Mom; he wanted to call her in from the waiting room. I said okay, but when she joined us, I clammed up. She looked so tense, so expectant, like she was paying Dr. Deadhead all this money and now she was here to collect. "My daughter's spent two hours with you; show me you've knocked some sense into her. Convince me you've made her perfect again."

I broke out in a cold sweat. I couldn't talk to her. I couldn't even look at her. So I started crying instead.

I put the journal on my chest as I lie in bed and listen to Mom on the phone in her bedroom. She's doing her dog-and-pony show for some hapless first-time house hunter. I'm catching only the tail end of the conversation, but I've heard it all before and already have the gist.

"Oh, it's perfect for you!" she coos. "Totally adorable! You know, my husband and I couldn't afford much when we first married, but wouldn't you know, we stumbled across the cutest little fixer-upper bungalow, and I tell you, it was the most charming place I've ever lived! Oh, I had such fun making my own curtains and putting little flower boxes in the windowsills! That's what this place reminds me of."

Mom's really good at her job. She sells lots of houses, really fancy ones in addition to the "fixer-upper bungalows" (read "shacks"). She doesn't care if she's selling something worth a million dollars or a fraction of that. She sees the potential in everything and helps other people see it, too. I gotta hand that to her.

Not that her success is any secret. Her face is on a dozen billboards throughout town *(Susanne Stetson holds the KEY to your HAPPINESS!)*, and half a dozen "Realtor of the Year" trophies are on the fireplace mantle. She used to drag me along on occasional open-house events, and I marveled at how long she could hold a fake smile.

I hear her hang up the phone and start another conversation.

"I have asked you a thousand times not to leave wet clothes in the dryer," she tells Dad in a brittle voice. "They sour."

Silence.

"Do you hear me, Randall? This is important!"

More silence.

I roll my eyes. How many of these kinds of conversations did Shannon overhear? I bet Mom made *her* head spin, too, with all her happy talk and fake smiles for the outside world, and all her nagging for Dad.

I pick the journal back up and read another entry.

Wednesday, June 16, 1993

Drum roll, please:

 I SAVED A LIFE TODAY!

 And on my very first day as a lifeguard!

 I'd just gotten to the pool, and even from the parking lot I could tell something was up. I heard screaming, then started running. When I got through the gate, I saw people gathered at the baby pool. Mary Ellen, the lifeguard with the early shift, was standing in the pool trying to jerk something out of the water. Several people were crying, and someone yelled to me, "She's stuck!"

 That's when I realized what was going on. A toddler's hair was stuck in the drain of the baby pool, and Mary Ellen was trying to yank her free. Mary Ellen looked like she was going to puke. The yanking obviously wasn't working, and the baby couldn't survive long under water.

 Long story about why I had scissors in my gym bag, but suffice it to say I'll never go to a pool again without a pair. I grabbed my scissors, dropped my gym bag to the ground, ran to the baby pool, jumped in, cut the little girl's hair and pulled her out of the water. She was already turning blue, so I laid her on the side of the pool and started doing CPR.

There must have been fifty people standing around me, either crying or screaming or yelling out instructions. The mom kept screaming, "Don't hurt her, don't hurt her!" But I tuned everybody out and concentrated on the little girl. After a few breaths and chest compressions, water started coming out of her mouth. I turned her to her side, and she almost immediately started coughing and crying. An ambulance showed up a few minutes later and took her to the hospital, just to be sure she was okay. The mom called later to thank me and tell me her little girl is fine. I told her I was just happy to help, and that she didn't even have to pay me for the haircut!

I set the journal down for a second a take a deep breath. Wow. Even in midst of Shannon's rebel act, she was still so ... awesome. It's always been easy for me to resent her trophies and awards. I never thought to actually admire them. I think about the Red Cross plaque that hangs on the Shannon Wall of Fame. Before, it was just one more item on an endless brag sheet. But now, it really *means* something. She learned CPR through that Red Cross course. She saved somebody's life with it. God, I've been so snotty about Shannon all my life.

"You," I tell myself out loud, "are an idiot."

I keep reading.

Thursday, June 17, 1993

No life-saving at the pool today! In fact, today was downright boring, other than people walking over to tell me how stupendous I was yesterday. (Please, please ... no autographs!)

One of those people was none other than Eve. She came to the pool and said she'd heard about what happened. At first it was kind of awkward, but then we loosened up and started talking and laughing like we used to. She asked me to come to her house after my shift ended. Her dad would grill burgers, her mom would pop popcorn and we could watch scary movies all night.

I told her sorry, it sounded great (it really kinda did!), but that Chris was meeting me after my shift. (I made her promise not to tell Mom.)

Anyway, I wish I'd taken her up on her offer, because OF COURSE Chris ended up having to help his dad fix a transmission on a truck. Or something like that. He promised he'd make it up to me, but here I sit, all alone with my journal and a killer sunburn, missing my sweetie and thinking that scary movies and popcorn don't sound half bad.

I put the journal aside, pick up my cell phone and call Gibs.

"Hi," he says.

"Hi. I'm gonna look up Shannon's friend, Eve."

Nineteen

Mothballs.

That's what I'm smelling. Even on the front porch, the odor hits me like a locomotive. I smile quickly to make my crinkled nose less obvious as a plump, gray-haired lady opens the front door.

"Mrs. Brice? Hi. Thanks for letting me stop by. I know my call was totally out of the blue..."

Eve's mother draws in a breath. "You look just like your sister," she says, then blinks hard as her eyes moisten.

She leads me into the living room of the ranch-style house. A sofa with celery-green upholstery sits against one wall, an upright piano against another. Two faded armchairs sit stiffly to one side, like soldiers guarding the room. A lamp on an end table casts a golden glow on Mrs. Brice's face as she guides me to the sofa and sits beside me. I smile at her, weakly. This lady is nice enough, but she seems so . . . ancient. No wonder Eve seems like such a priss in Shannon's journal. Her mother is right out of schoolmarm central casting.

"You look *just like her*!" she repeats, putting her hand on my knee. I hear this a lot, but never quite like this. Mrs. Brice is acting like she's seeing a ghost.

"Shannon was way prettier than me," I say, then swallow hard and blush. Could I sound any more pathetic?

"No!" Mrs. Brice insists. "The resemblance is remarkable."

I glance at the piano.

"Do you play?"

Mrs. Brice crinkles her brow, then nods vigorously. "Yes! And I teach. I taught Shannon!"

My throat catches. I knew Shannon played, but I never pictured her *learning* to play. My sister is always fully formed in my imagination. "You taught her here?" I ask.

Mrs. Brice nods and her eyes soften. "Right in this very room. Thursdays at four. I must have taught her for—goodness—seven years or so, at least until she started high school, maybe even a year or so after that. She was very good. She'd learned a Rachmaninoff piece by the time she was nine! She was so disciplined; I can see her now, staring at the keys so intently and playing with such passion. Truly, one of the most gifted students I've ever had."

I stare at the piano bench, imagining my sister sitting there, poised and purposeful.

"And you?" Mrs. Brice says. "Do you play?"

My eyes stay planted on the piano bench for a long moment. "I took lessons for a couple of years, but... no." I wonder why I didn't take lessons from *her*. Maybe she's wondering the same thing.

A silent moment lingers, then Mrs. Brice lays a hand on top of mine. "Your sister was a wonderful girl."

My eyes lock with hers. "She and Eve were best friends, right?" I ask her.

She nods decisively and folds her hands primly in her lap. "Since second grade. Inseparable, those two. They were Brownies together, then Girl Scouts—always side by side throughout all their little clubs and activities."

"But then they drifted apart," I prod.

Mrs. Brice looks confused, then waves away the suggestion. "Why would you say that? They were always very close."

I sigh. Do mothers know *anything*?

"I think they started to grow apart a few months before Shannon died," I say tentatively. "Shannon started dating a guy Eve didn't like."

Mrs. Brice blushes and looks at her lap. "I think I did hear something about that."

"From Eve? Did she talk about it?"

Mrs. Brice's eyelids flutter. She looks... annoyed?

"Of course she talked about it," she says defensively. "But their spat... it was nothing. They would have patched things up if..."

She intertwines her fingers.

"Honey, I don't know exactly what you're trying to find

out," she says after an awkward moment. "But there was no big drama involving their relationship. They were wonderful friends who went through a rough patch. That's all. I'm sure Eve mentioned things to me here and there, but I wasn't concerned."

She shifts her weight to face me squarely. "Your sister may have gone through some growing pains—dating a fellow who wasn't really right for her and whatnot—but that wasn't *her*. It was clear to everybody who knew Shannon that she would be a wonderful success in life, even if she stumbled a little—just a little—along the way. I mean, my heavens, she was playing Rachmaninoff at nine!"

My eyes drift toward the sunlight streaming through a bay window.

"Did she ever talk about my mom?" I ask.

"*Talk* about her? Well, I suppose she did, but she and Eve were busy playing Barbies and practicing their cheers, not talking about their mothers. Besides, Shannon couldn't tell me anything about your mother I didn't already know. We were constantly doing things together. We were great friends."

I eye Mrs. Brice guardedly. "Then why don't you and Mom still see each other?"

She blushes. She begins to speak, but her voice catches and she starts over. "I feel terrible about that," she says. "I did try to keep up with Susanne for a while after ... after the accident ... but I almost felt cruel being around her. Here was Eve, graduating from high school, moving on with her life ... I would have felt like I was rubbing that in her face. Then, when you came along, I thought, 'Perfect. Fresh start. Susanne gets to have all the joys of mother-hood again.' I didn't want to intrude on that. I didn't want to be a constant reminder of the past."

She worries her necklace and looks out the window. "Like I said, I feel terrible." She turns toward me. "How is your mother doing, Summer?"

"She's okay...she's fine. Did she and Shannon get along?"

Mrs. Brice's eyes flash confusion. "Of *course*, Summer. They got along beautifully. Why wouldn't they?"

It's official—this woman is clueless.

"I guess every mother-daughter relationship has its challenges," she continues. "But I never saw a problem in the world between those two. Oh, we had such fun together. We'd alternate houses for trick-or-treating, and we always made ornaments and cookies together at Christ-mas. Of course, we were always running the girls around to their various club meetings or fundraising projects. I think one was sleeping over at the other's practically every weekend."

I realize I have a faint smile. *This* is the Shannon my family keeps alive, the little girl making Christmas orna-ments or having bake sales for cheerleading camp. But the thought of Shannon's journal jolts me back to reality.

"So it must have been weird when Shannon and Eve stopped hanging out together."

Now Mrs. Brice definitely looks annoyed. "They didn't stop *hanging out*," she says testily, using air quotes. "They were just getting older, staying busy. It was nothing. Why are you asking about this anyway, dear?"

My lashes flicker against the late-afternoon sunlight, which is getting harsher by the minute as it streams through the bay window. "She kept a journal the summer before she died." I swallow hard. "I'm reading it."

"Ah." Mrs. Brice fingers her necklace again. "She wrote about her friendship with Eve?"

I nod. "Nothing bad," I emphasize. "Eve's great. I can tell by reading the journal."

"Mmmmm," Mrs. Brice says.

I pull a lock of hair behind my ear and sit up straighter. "Mrs. Brice, I'm sorry to pop up out of nowhere and ask you personal questions. I don't mean to freak you out. I'm not implying there was some great mystery or something. I know friends can grow apart. I just…"

"Eve sang at her funeral," Mrs. Brice says evenly, her chin jutting forward subtly. "They had *not* grown apart."

My shoulders sink. "Right."

A tense moment passes, then Mrs. Brice's expression softens. She leans closer, her very pores smelling of mothballs. "Would you like to talk to Eve?"

Twenty

Friday, June 18, 1993
Oh. My. God.

I got home from my shift at the pool this afternoon and Mom told me to hurry and change, we were having guests for dinner.

Grandma and Grandpa? I asked.

Uh … yeah. And they were bringing some friends.

So I went upstairs, took a shower, changed into shorts and T-shirt and came back down, wondering which geriatric Knights of Columbus couple was showing up.

My first clue should have been when Mom shooed me back upstairs, telling me I wasn't dressed nicely enough. She told me to put on a dress, or at least "some nice slacks." And to comb my hair again. Oh, and not to forget the mouthwash.

The upshot: Yes, the guests were part of the Knights of Columbus clan, but they didn't come empty-handed. They brought their GRANDSON. It was a fix-up!

MORTIFYING!!!

I had to choke down my mashed potatoes while Chad, a guy with (how to say this kindly) an unfortunate complexion and an even more unfortunate plaid shirt, yammered on for an hour about the senior cruise he just got back from.

A senior cruise with other high school seniors? No. A senior cruise with his grandparents.

The thought of Plaid Chad playing shuffleboard with a bunch of senior citizens with cataracts, fallen arches, and liver spots didn't exactly whisk me away to Romance City.

I thought, what with him being on senior time, he might have to call it a night by seven and head on home for a good night's sleep, but no, he stayed through three servings of peach cobbler, seven rounds of charades, and a hundred and forty-eight mentions of his almost-perfect score on the math section of his SAT.

When it was my turn for charades, he was the first to guess the movie I was acting out ("Better Off Dead") but the last to catch my drift. I think even his grandparents were catching on that Plaid Chad's *best shot at romance had probably sailed away with the widows on the cruise. Mom kept tossing me stern be-nice-to-Chad looks, but by the time he was acting out The Love Boat in charades, I think she was ready to toss him overboard, too.*

When Chad asked for my phone number as they were finally calling it a night, it was Mom who told him what a busy, busy summer I was having, that I really didn't have time for socializing, that I had to spend the summer preparing for my own SAT, but gosh, what a lovely young man he was and what a pleasant evening we'd all enjoyed.

She shut the door behind them, then looked at me like I was a caged tiger that had just jumped the fence. Her expression was so intense, I couldn't help laughing. Then Mom started laughing, too. Pretty soon we were holding our sides, we were laughing so hard.

That's the first time we've laughed together in a long time.

I was still laughing when I called Chris to tell him about it. I figured he'd crack up too, but instead he got all moody and mad, like he was jealous of Plaid Chad. Isn't that crazy? I reassure him all the time that I want to spend every second of the rest of my life with him, that he's the ONLY man for me, but he's still really insecure. Sometimes it feels really flattering, and sometimes it feels just kinda... I don't know. Just kinda whatever.

Oh, well. I'll make it up to Chris tomorrow
when I make us a spectacular picnic lunch. Chad is
not invited.

I tap my finger idly against the journal and smile into space.

I love the thought of Mom and Shannon laughing together. My bedroom door is open, so I glance from my bed into the hallway at her awards and certificates hanging on the wall. I've been so consumed lately with the bad-ass Shannon that it's a relief to be reintroduced to the Shannon I knew before I started reading her journal—the one who smiled and laughed, even with Mom. *Especially* with Mom. My stomach tightens at the thought of how hard it must have been for Mom when Shannon started pushing her away.

But she *had* to push Mom away, to keep from suffocating.

And of course, once she pushed Mom away, idiot Chris was right there to pick up where Mom left off.

Brilliant, Shannon, way to bounce from one control freak to another, I think wryly. Why couldn't she see what a loser Chris was?

I reach for my cell phone, then curse under my breath. Gibs has been out of town all week building houses for Habitat for Humanity. Whatever little rural corner of the state he's in is a dead zone; none of my calls have gone through. Jeez, I'd love to talk to him right now.

Maybe now is a good time to call Eve. I programmed

her number into my phone as soon as Mrs. Brice gave it to me, but I haven't quite been able to make the call. Is it just the sheer awkwardness of talking to a total stranger? Maybe...but that's not the only thing holding me back. The closer I get to Shannon as a real-live person, the farther I get from the dazzling persona I've lived with all my life. Maybe I'm not quite willing to let it go yet. But who am I kidding? Shannon's dazzle gets dimmer with every journal entry. I sigh and keep reading:

Saturday, June 19, 1993

My dad did the most random thing tonight. He came into my room after I'd gone to bed and sat there staring at me until I opened my eyes. I gasped when I saw him; I'd already drifted off to sleep, and he scared me to death. But he squeezed my hand and told me it was okay; it was just Daddy.

Then he reached in his pocket and pulled out a box. He couldn't look me in the eye when he handed it to me, but he mumbled that he wanted me to have it. I sat up, turned on my bedside lamp and opened the box.

It was a necklace. Topaz. Dad said it reminded him of the flecks in my eyes. I asked him what the occasion was, and he said no occasion, just a way to remind me that he loved me. I said thanks and he helped me fasten the clasp behind my neck.

Then Dad did something I've never seen him do before: he started crying. Not bawling or anything,

*just crying, really softly. I wanted to comfort him,
but I was so freaked out, I couldn't bring myself to
give him a hug. I leaned back against my pillow
while he dabbed his eyes.*

*He swallowed hard, then told me he was sorry
he'd disappointed me. He wanted to be perfect for
me. He wanted to be my hero. He was sorry he was
such a failure.*

*I was clutching my topaz stone so tightly I
thought it might crumble in my fingers. A zillion
times, I'd cried myself to sleep wishing Dad and I
could have a real conversation, but now that we were
having one, I couldn't handle it. I could barely even
look at him.*

*All the questions I wanted to ask him got caught
in my throat: "How could you hurt Mom that way?"
"How could you be such a hypocrite, telling me how
to live while you sneaked around behind our backs?"
"Why weren't Mom and I enough for you?"*

*All those years, I'd thought doing the right thing
came naturally to Dad, that he was happy to be a
good guy. But no, the right thing was a struggle, a
hassle, a bother. I guess I was a bother, too.*

*He seemed to read my mind, because he told me
that Mom and I had always made him happy, that
we were more than he deserved.*

Then why?

Because I'm an idiot, he said.

Was she the first one? I asked.

He nodded, but he couldn't look me in the eye.

Then my eyes filled with tears and I squeezed my topaz so hard I must have accidentally yanked the chain. It broke. The stone slid off the chain and disappeared. We spent a couple of minutes looking for it, but it was gone.

Maybe it'll turn up one day. Or maybe it's gone forever.

———————

My chin trembles as I close the journal. Dad *did* talk to Shannon.

Gibs is right: *I'm* the one who doesn't want to talk about things. I'm the biggest coward in the family.

My gaze skims out the door, down the hall toward Shannon's old bedroom. I feel a desperate urge to run into the room, get on my hands and knees, and scour every square inch of the carpet in search of that topaz stone.

But I'd never find it. Besides, it isn't mine to find.

I push my face into my pillow and cry myself to sleep.

Twenty-One

Monday, June 21, 1993

Dr. Deadhead wants to meet Dad.

He thinks the fact that he finally got real with me indicates he's ready to take our relationship to a new level, a genuine level, an authentic level where we can see each other as real people and quit playing roles.

I told Dr. Deadhead I'm afraid if I quit playing a role, I'll disintegrate. I AM my role, I told him. He said he didn't believe it, that he could tell I was finally finding my true self.

Like how I'm finally choosing real friendships with people like Jamie? I asked him.

"Now THAT'S a role," he said with a laugh, and I asked him what the hell that meant.

I'm playing the bad girl, he said, overcompensating for the nauseating goody-goody I've always been. When Jamie and I sneak off to smoke pot, I'm not being my true self. I'm being Teen Rebel straight out of central casting. But that's okay, he told me. I probably need to try on some different roles before I finally get comfortable in my own skin. Just as long as I don't do anything too stupid.

Jamie's a real person, I told him, not just a prop in my life.

But it isn't the real Jamie I'm interested in, he told me. Just the part of Jamie I can use as a springboard to escape the suffocation of a fake-perfect life.

So I'm using Jamie?

Well…yeah, he said.

Except that I'm not. She's a true friend.

You're sure about that? Dr. Deadhead asked me.

YES!

And Chris? Dr. Deadhead said. You're totally yourself in that relationship, too?

Uh, duh. I'm in love with Chris.

Mmmmmm, Dr. Deadhead said.

Okay, I said, I'll humor you. Let's assume I'm faking it with Chris. How will I know when I'm being real in a relationship?

When you don't have to defend the person you love, he said. When you don't need to sneak around.

It isn't because our love's not real that we

sneak around, I told him. It's because my mom is a judgmental, social-climbing control freak.

Which is when he said it was a good time to call Mom in to join us.

But I said no. Mom and I had actually laughed together the other day. It felt good. If she came in now, we'd both freak out.

Dr. Deadhead asked if I could bear a little tension if it meant I could feel closer to my mother.

I told him I don't think I can get closer to her, that the better she knows me, the less she'll love me.

He doesn't believe it, but I do. Dr. Deadhead may be brilliant, but I know my mom better than he does.

I begged him not to call her in. Not this time. Not this day.

He stared at me a long time, then said okay.

Maybe next time.

"I met with Eve's mother."

Gibs gives me a blank look. "Eve," he finally says. It's a question, not a statement.

"*Shannon's best friend,*" I snap.

"Oh, right." He dips a tortilla chip into his salsa and bites off the tip.

"*Oh, right?*" I say in a steely voice. "That's all you have to say?"

Gibs considers my question as he chews. "How did it go?" he asks after he swallows.

I push my burrito around on the paper plate with my plastic fork. "It went ... weird."

Gibs eats another chip. "How so?"

I shrug sullenly.

Gibs returned from his Habitat trip after midnight last night, so grabbing burritos with him on my lunch break is the first chance I've had to talk to him in days. I have so much information built up—Shannon's visits with her shrink, her heart-to-heart with Dad, my meeting with Mrs. Brice—but Gibs barely seems interested.

"You act like you don't care," I mutter, still picking at my burrito.

Gibs looks at me evenly. "I care."

I peek at him. "Ya sure?"

He nods. "I guess I'm just tired."

My feel my eyes soften. "Oh, right. Habitat." I force a smile. "How did it go?"

He sips his soft drink. "Good. It counts toward my IB volunteer hours, you know. Plus it was actually a lot of fun. We built four houses in seven days."

I give a low whistle. "That's a lot of hammering."

He shrugs. "It was a lot of work, but—"

"Do you want to hear about Mrs. Brice?"

Gibs sighs. "I don't know. I'd rather talk about you than about Shannon."

I frown. "What do you mean?"

"I don't know. Nothing. Whatever."

I huff impatiently. "What are you talking about?"

He stares at his fingers. "When you build houses with Habitat, you build them alongside of the people who will be living there. You know—people who are really down on their luck, out of options. It makes you attuned to how lucky we are."

"Deep."

Gibs glances at me, but he pushes past my sarcasm. "There are a lot of people out there who need help," he says.

My shoulders tense. "Your point?"

His eyes skirt past me again. "Maybe we should live in the moment more. "You seem kinda...over the top with your sister's journal."

My eyes narrow. "*Over the top.*" It's a question, not a statement.

He leans into his elbows. "Maybe just a little. I know it's intense, learning new things about your sister, but..."

"*Learning new things,*" I repeat, my eyes narrowed to slits.

Gibs sighs in defeat.

I shake my head roughly. "I'm not learning new things. I'm *meeting* her, Gibs, for the first time. I'm getting to know my sister. You said it yourself: a sister isn't like some random relative, or some long-dead ancestor. Jesus, *you're* the one who encouraged me to read her journal! And to realize she struggled with some of the same crap I deal with..." *And did I mention, my sister may have committed suicide?*

Gibs glances anxiously around the restaurant, then locks eyes with mine. "I just ... worry about you, you know?" he says in barely a whisper. "Maybe we could talk about the present sometimes. I mean, it's summer. You should be having at least a little fun."

I gaze at him evenly. "This coming from the guy who just spent a week installing drywall."

A look of anger flashes in his dark blue eyes. "Excuse me for thinking about somebody besides myself," he says in a clipped voice.

I gasp a little. I've never seen Gibs angry before.

My first instinct is to apologize, to acknowledge what a self-absorbed moron I've been. To say, *Don't you know that your opinion of me is the only one in the whole world that I care about, and by the way, why don't you get how much I'm starting to like you?*

But no, that would require being vulnerable, and I've learned from the Ice Queen herself that *that* will never do. So I set my jaw instead.

"Like I need a reminder of how perfect you are," I say icily.

Gibs leans closer, holding my gaze steadily. "I never said I was perfect."

"Oh, please."

He tosses his hand in the air. "God, Summer, you give all this lip service to how much you hate labels, how you're all about individuality, but you put people in boxes all the time."

My eyes are narrowed to slits, which usually has a chilling effect on conversations, but Gibs isn't finished yet.

"Maybe I don't want to be in one of your goddamn boxes," he says.

He gives me a second to respond, but I'm too busy glaring to speak.

So he walks out.

———

Tears sting my eyes, but I squeeze them tightly to staunch the flow. The only thing more pathetic than sitting alone in a Taco Primo booth is sitting alone in a Taco Primo booth crying.

I grab a tortilla chip from the basket and chomp on it angrily.

What just happened? I've been counting the days to seeing Gibs, but when we're finally together, he bites my head off.

Okay, maybe it isn't quite that simple. For one thing, I'm only just acknowledging to *myself* how much I dig him, so there's no reason for him to guess my little secret. But that whole five-year plan I have? The one about us reconnecting down the road when we're ready for a relationship? Screw that. I want Gibs to care about me *now*.

And speaking of caring—does he have to rub it in my face that I'm apparently the least caring, least competent, least worthy individual on earth? Particularly when compared to my life-saving sister and my house-building best friend?

I choke down my tortilla chip, then pick up another. But I throw it back into the basket in disgust and stomp out of the restaurant.

Twenty-Two

"Uh...Summer?"

I lay a pile of asters on the work table and wipe my hands on the seat of my jeans. "Yep," I call, then walk to the front of the store to see what Aunt Nic needs.

I freeze in my tracks as I approach the cash register. Aunt Nic's standing there, looking confused, and Gibs is on the other side of the counter with a fistful of daisies.

"O-*kay*," I say as I join them.

"He *brought* flowers," Aunt Nic clarifies. "That's got to be a first—somebody bringing flowers to a flower shop."

I hesitate, then swallow hard and join them. Gibs hands me the daisies shyly, making a peace sign with his free hand.

"Aunt Nic, you remember my friend Gibs. He ate Japanese with us on my birthday."

She smiles warmly. "Yeah, sure. Hi, Gibs. Um…didn't you two just have lunch together?"

Gibs nods and shifts his weight nervously. "We did, actually. I just thought I'd drop these by. I was in the neighborhood. Nice to see you again, Mrs.…."

He extends his hand and Aunt Nic shakes it. "Nic," she tells him. "Just call me Nic."

He nods, but he can't spit it out, so he keeps quiet.

"Well," Aunt Nic says, wiping her hands together briskly. "I've got some flower-arranging to do." She flutters her fingertips at us, then walks toward the work room.

"Flowers," I say to Gibs.

He stuffs his hands in the pockets of his shorts and stares at his sneakers. "Yeah. A peace offering. I wasn't even thinking about this being a flower shop. But I guess that would've been kinda weird…buying flowers from you, then handing them back to you."

I bite my lower lip.

"I'm sorry I walked out," he says, his eyes searching mine.

I lay the daisies on the counter and steal a glance at him. "I thought calling you 'perfect' was a compliment," I say.

He sputters with laughter, then I laugh, too. Finally, our eyes are locked.

"I'm the one who's sorry," I say. "I know I can be a total asshole. And you're right: I *am* a little obsessed with Shannon."

Gibs shakes his head. "I totally get it."

I finger a lock of my hair. "I like being able to talk to you about it, you know? I mean, I can talk to Aunt Nic, but she's a part of it. *You*...I don't have to worry about hurting you."

A silent moment passes.

"Thanks for the flowers," I say. "It was really sweet."

He smiles as he scans the shop, flowers springing from practically every square inch of the room. "Chocolates next time," he says.

"Good plan."

He bounces on the balls of his feet and raises his eyebrows. "Hey, speaking of fun..."

I put a hand on my hip. "We were speaking of fun?"

"Yeah. That whole 'Sure, read Shannon's journal, but have some fun this summer, too'—that whole thread—"

I giggle at him.

"Um, I was just wondering," Gibs continues, rubbing a lightly stubbled chin, "and I totally understand if it doesn't work out, I mean what with your job and all, and whatever else you have going on, but if you *were* able to get away for a few days, and, you know, that whole idea of squeezing in some fun, um..."

"*What?*" I prod.

"Well...my folks have a place at the beach. Nothing fancy, just a...you know, a place."

I nod. "A place."

"Yeah. A place. At the beach. Anyway, we're going there for a week...kind of a Fourth of July getaway...well, not really a getaway, just a...just a little trip. And anyway,

I was thinking, 'Hey, I was just telling Summer she could use a little fun,' and I called my mom, and she said sure, invite her, so if you don't have anything else to do, you know, if you could take a few days off work, and if you *wanted* to, no pressure or anything, but if a few days at the beach might be fun, then I was wondering…"

I know I should throw him a lifeline by saying something, anything, but he's so cute when he's nervous.

"You're inviting me to the beach," I say after he sputters to a halt.

He considers what I've just said, then nods.

Still holding his gaze, I call, "Hey, Aunt Nic, can I have a few days off around the Fourth for a trip to the beach?"

"Sure," she calls.

"Okay," I tell Gibs. "Thanks."

He considers my words again, then nods sharply. "Okay, then. Good. Great, really. I mean, I'm glad you can come."

"I have to check with my mom, of course, but…"

"Of course," Gibs says, making me giggle by sounding like a high school principal. "And your mom can call my mom. Whatever she needs to do. And if it works out, well…" He claps his hands together. "Well, great."

I study him evenly. "I'll certainly do everything in my power to expedite the arrangements," I say, and he blushes when he realizes I'm making fun of him.

He rubs the back of his neck. "Yeah, well… I'd better let you get back to work."

"Right," I say. "Work."

He smiles and waves.

"Hey, Gibs," I call as he walks toward the door.

He turns around. "Yeah?"

"Thanks for the flowers. And the beach trip. It sounds great."

He gives a little salute that makes me giggle some more, then walks out the door.

It's ridiculous how my stomach is doing somersaults. Is it possible Gibs is into me? That he's ready to fast-forward my five-year plan? I mean, a beach trip, even if it *is* with his parents... that has real relationship potential, right?

"Hmmmmm," Aunt Nic says.

I jump, not realizing she's rejoined me at the counter.

"Flowers?" Aunt Nic muses. "And a trip to the beach? He's got it bad."

I roll my eyes. "He's a friend. Just a friend."

She shakes her head. "Flowers aren't a friend thing." I shrug, then blush when I realize I have a ridiculous smile on my face.

"Think Mom will mind if I go to the beach with him?"

Aunt Nic shrugs. "If the private investigator's report comes up clean and Gibs' DNA doesn't match up with the FBI database, I'm sure she'll be cool with it."

"Funny."

"Oh, I was teasing?" She tousles my hair. "I better get you a vase for those daisies."

Twenty-Three

Wednesday, June 30, 1993
I think I have a sister.

I gasp and blink hard. *I think I have a sister.*

It's been four days since I last picked up Shannon's journal, and I still haven't called Eve. I guess Gibs' words made an impression on me. But with a whole leisurely Sunday stretching out ahead of me when I woke up this morning, I reached for the journal without giving it a thought.

And when I read the first sentence of the entry, I bolted upright in bed.

My eyes refocus on her words.

I know it sounds crazy, but God, I feel it so strongly.
I've felt it all my life. I remember asking Mom

when I was still in preschool whether she'd ever had another baby ... a miscarriage, a stillbirth, whatever. I didn't use those words, of course; I was just rooting around for an explanation. I FELT a sister, like you feel someone's breath on the back of your neck.

A chill ripples up my spine and I lightly run my finger along the paper.

When Mom said no, that I was her only child, my imagination went into overdrive. I was adopted. That was the only possible explanation. I'd spend hours adding details: my real mom lived at the beach raising my sister, trying to put on a brave front but pacing the beach night after night, staring into the moon and pining away for me.

Why had she given me away? My versions varied. She was a teenager, a musical prodigy who would lose her scholarship to Julliard if she kept me. Or she was a soap opera actress in New York City whose career would be doomed by a baby. Or she had cruel parents who had ripped me from her arms the night I was born and laid me on the steps of Mom's church.

Any of the versions suited me. She was impossibly beautiful and she'd never wanted to give me away, but fate had played its hand. So now she dreamed of me, wept for me, obsessed about me, devoted her life to finding me and bringing me home. Home to her

*and my sister. (A twin? An identical twin? The one
her cruel parents had allowed her to keep?)*

*My "real" father never factored into my fantasy.
Isn't that funny?*

*As I got older, the fantasy fell apart. I look an
awful lot like my mother, and everybody's stories are
pretty consistent about Mom's thirty-six-hour labor,
and the tongs the doctor used to pull me out of the
birth canal, and how I'd come out smiling anyway,
and how I'd spit up all over the pearl-white gown
my grandma had smocked for my trip home from the
hospital.*

*Besides, half the girls in my elementary school
insisted they'd been given up at birth by their real
moms (theirs were beautiful, too) and they were
resigned to making do with the schlumpy women
who slapped together the PB&Js for their lunchboxes
every morning.*

*I loved my fantasy and hated realizing it was a
dime a dozen. I wanted to snap off the heads of my
friends who prattled on about their stupid adoption
fantasies. "So let me get this straight: Your real mom
is Madonna, but you somehow look uncannily like
Elmer Fudd?"*

*MY fantasy, even after it fell apart, was different.
I've never stopped feeling my sister's breath on the back
of my neck.*

*Now that I know about Dad's affair, I can't help
wondering if THAT'S the explanation. He says it*

was his only affair, but was it really? Does he have another daughter out there somewhere?

This explanation is more complicated, all messy and tacky. It's the explanation that has me doing double-takes on sidewalks and in the mall, trying to detect a glimmer of my genes in girls trying on perfume at Victoria's Secret.

I guess it's possible, but it doesn't feel right. My sister isn't some clueless twit with vacant eyes chomping gum with her mouth wide open in aisle seven at Kroger.

She's . . . spectacular. I know it. I feel it.

Who are you, sister? Are you really out there?

Do you feel me, too?

The journal drops on my lap and the lump in my throat finally dislodges. I remind myself to breathe. My cell phone rings and I jump.

"Hello?" I say cautiously.

"What's wrong?" Gibs asks.

Tears sting my eyes. "Can I meet you at the park?"

———

"She knew about me," I say quietly, sitting in the grass with my knees pushed into my chest. "She says in her journal that she knew she had a sister."

Pause. "I don't get it," Gibs replies.

I pick up the journal. I've never read him any entries

before—just paraphrased. Somehow I haven't wanted to share her actual words with anybody, including Gibs. But now I'm tempted to read what she wrote. I skim the pages and turn to the beginning of the entry and open my mouth.

I can't do it. I can talk *about* Shannon to him, but I'm not ready to share her words ... particularly considering what they might ultimately be leading to.

"I don't think she was psychic or anything," I finally say. "She just says she felt like she had a sister. All her life she'd felt that way. When she was little, she wondered if she was adopted. Then she wondered if Dad had, like, a love child out there somewhere. Because she knew she had a sister, Gibs."

"But she *didn't* have a sister," Gibs says sensibly. "You weren't born until after she died. So whatever sister she was fantasizing about couldn't have been you."

I shake my head. "I don't think our connection has anything to do with time or space. It's deeper than that."

I pluck a dandelion from the ground and watch its tendrils disperse in a light breeze. "It's like she knew I would read her journal one day," I say, still gazing at the dandelion.

"Okay," Gibs says.

"Do you believe in God?" I ask him abruptly, facing him head on.

He shrugs. "I don't know."

I press my lips together. "I don't either. But the connection I feel to Shannon ... the connection *she* felt to *me* ... I can't explain it."

I let the bald dandelion fall from my fingers and pluck another one from the ground.

"I wish she was still alive. It would change everything."

Gibs waves a dandelion tendril from his face. "What would be different?"

I shrug. "You know me. I'm kind of a dud in the friend department. I mean, I had girlfriends when I was younger—Leah Rollins, Priscilla Pratt, whoever—but even when we hung around together as little kids, I always felt like an outsider. Then, when they started obsessing over makeup and highlights . . . we had nothing in common at that point." I lean back onto the palms of my hands, the cool, moist grass seeping through my fingertips. "Shannon could have been my best friend."

Gibs cocks his head slightly. "You might not have been friends at all. You might have driven each other crazy. Lots of sisters do."

I squint into his eyes, the white sun hitting my face like a spotlight. "No. We would have understood each other. We would have been the only ones who *could* understand each other."

"Maybe," Gibs says. "But who cares if you don't have girlfriends? You have me."

My heart leaps a little.

"What difference does it make whether your best friend is a girl or a guy?" he continues. "A friend is a friend."

I dig my fingers deeper into the squishy grass. *Quit being my friend, Gibs. Friendship isn't enough for me anymore.*

"Hey, have you thought about where you're going to college?" I ask him impulsively. "I'm guessing Harvard…"

He nods. Oh. I thought I was kidding.

"That's my first choice," he says. "But it's tough to get in." He hesitates, then says, "How about you?"

I toss a hand in the air. "Yeah, I'm thinking Harvard is my first choice, too."

He laughs, which is what I was going for, but for some reason makes me really sad. Why have I been such a screw-up in school all these years? Was being the anti-Shannon really such a great idea?

"I did pretty well on the SAT," I tell him, then feel embarrassed by how lame that sounds.

His expression turns earnest. "I'm sure you did. I know how smart you are."

I sit up straighter and rest my chin on my hand. "I've been stupid for blowing off school all these years, haven't I?"

Gibs' eyes look gentle. "You'll make up for lost time when you figure out what you want to do."

I pinch my lips together. "Yeah, but I'll be figuring it out at Morton Community College while you're in pre-med at Harvard."

He leans closer to me. "We'll stay friends, no matter where we go to college."

Friends. Beach trip or no beach trip, I don't think Gibs is ready to step things up a notch.

I squint into the sunlight. "Did I tell you Shannon saved a life when she was a lifeguard? Some kid's hair got stuck in the kiddie pool drain. She cut her loose, then did CPR."

"Wow," Gibs says.

I nod. "Pretty cool, huh? I mean, in some ways she seems really naïve and immature to me, then *bang*, she's saving a kid's life."

He nods thoughtfully.

A breeze blows through my hair. "You know when I called you perfect, and it made you so mad?" I say. "I didn't mean to sound snotty. It's just that I'm really ... disappointed in myself, you know?"

I try to look away, but he's holding my gaze.

"I think you're amazing," he says firmly.

Birds chirp and toddlers chatter in the background.

I think I love you, I tell him telepathically.

He gets that, right?

Maybe not. Maybe one day I'll start saying what I'm thinking.

Twenty-Four

Mom is weeding her flower bed when I pull into the driveway.

She waves as I get out of the car. I walk over and sit on the grass, careful to avoid her impatiens. She glances up at me and looks startled.

"Hi!" she says, then peers anxiously at my white shorts. "You sure you want to be sitting in the grass? You'll stain your clothes."

I shrug. "I just got back from sitting in the grass at the park. Guess I'm stain-proof now."

"Who were you at the park with?"

"Gibs."

"Mmmmmm. Oh, incidentally, I talked to his mother about the beach trip. She seems like a lovely person."

"Yeah, his folks are great."

Mom looks at me closer. "And Gibs? Do you think Gibs is great, too?"

"We're just friends."

"Mmmmmmm."

I study Mom's face as she resumes clawing into the crumbly black soil. This is when she looks prettiest to me: no makeup, even a little dirt smeared onto her cheeks, her fine wrinkles as distinct in the late-afternoon sunshine as the etched lines on a relief map. She hates her wrinkles, her pale lashes, the dark shadows under her eyes; she spends forever in front of the mirror each morning camouflaging her face with makeup. But this is how I like her best.

She glances at me again and seems to read her mind, putting a hand self-consciously against her cheek.

"I look like something the cat dragged in," she says.

"Mom, what happened to the friends you had when Shannon was alive?" I ask.

She resumes digging in the dirt. It's the first time she hasn't acted startled when I've mentioned Shannon's name.

"What friends?" she asks.

"Your friends. People you sang with in the choir at church. Your book club friends. The mothers of Shannon's friends."

She wrings a stubborn weed from the earth. "People come and go in life, Summer," she says without looking at me.

"So where did they go?"

She sighs and looks at me evenly. "Any particular friends you're interested in?"

I shrug. "I just think it's weird that the mom I know is

so different from the mom Shannon knew. I mean…your personality's the same, I guess, and God, your control-freak vibe is still going strong…"

Mom raises an eyebrow, but smiles. "*Gosh*, Summer," she chides me. "Say *gosh*, not *God*."

"…but friends don't just drop off the face of the earth," I continue. "Why'd you stop hanging with them?"

Mom wipes the back of her hand across her forehead, then sits next to me. "We never exactly *hung*," she says, her hands draped lazily across her knees.

I laugh at her, and she laughs back. "No, you're definitely not the type that hangs." I pluck a grass blade and run it between my fingers. "Do people dump you when your kid dies?" I ask impulsively.

I'm hoping for another laugh, but no such luck. Mom stares at her impatiens. "Actually, yes," she says in a faraway voice.

I inch closer to her. "That totally sucks," I say softly.

Mom shrugs. "It wasn't just them. It was me, too." She's still gazing at the flowers. "Everything changed after Shannon died. I wasn't the same person. I didn't care about books anymore, or tennis, or choir. And my friends? If our kids were the only thing we really had in common, well, where did that leave us?"

My jaw sets. "How could they dump you when you needed them most?" I ask in a steely voice.

Mom waves her hand absently. "They called, honey. They brought food. They invited me to movies…well, those first few weeks anyway. But they didn't know what to say, and I didn't know what I wanted them to say, and nothing would ever be the same again, and we all knew it, so…"

"You must have felt so alone," I say, a stiff breeze buffeting our faces.

"I had your father," she reminds me. "And Aunt Nicole, and the rest of our family." Her face brightens. "Then *you.* I got pregnant almost right away, you know, just weeks after she died."

Mom looks at me squarely. "You saved my life."

A chill runs up my spine. I've heard this all my life, usually from other people: *You gave your mother a reason to go on,* they say, or *I don't think she could have made it without you.* No pressure there, right?

I squeeze the blade of grass and green moisture stains my fingers. "It freaks me out a little when you say that, Mom."

Anger flashes across Mom's face.

"I mean, I'm glad you were happy to get pregnant again," I clarify, trying to sound casual. "It's just…" *It's just friggin' hard to be born with a job.*

"You don't have to explain," Mom says, her voice steely.

"Don't get mad, Mom," I say. "We should be able to talk about things."

"We're talking," she snaps.

I stand up abruptly and put my hands on my hips. "I hate it when you do this—shutting me out every time I try to open up to you."

Mom turns defiantly, returning to her hands and knees, returning to her weeds.

"By all means, Summer, open up and let me know it annoys you to be told you make me happy," she mutters to the dirt.

My stomach tightens and my eyes shimmer with tears. God. I never cry in front of my mother. "I'm not goddamn annoyed!"

Mom turns and stares at me sharply. "Don't curse at me, young lady."

I open my mouth to respond, but Mom has resumed digging in the dirt, clawing her fingers into the soil, yanking up weeds and tossing them aside without giving them another glance. Each weed will be purged methodically, systematically, impassively, until her garden is perfect.

And she is finished talking to me.

———

"I hate her!"

I bury my face in my hands. I was a ball of hot, indignant rage as I drove to Gibs' house, but now that I'm sitting with him in his den, my fury has melted into tears. They stream down my cheeks.

"Your mom?" Gibs surmises.

I rub my face with my fists. "She hasn't changed a bit! Poor Shannon—she went through all that shit for nothing. Mom didn't learn anything."

Gibs runs his fingers through his hair and reaches out to

touch me, but drops his hand before it reaches me. "What was she supposed to have learned?" he asks softly.

"How to quit being a control freak! A prissy, perfectionist, cold, callous control freak! It ruined my sister. Dad ruined her, too, good ol' don't-make-waves Dad, letting Mom call all the shots. *'Yes, dear,' 'Okay, dear,' 'Whatever, dear,'* sleepwalking through life except for his occasional fling with the church secretary…"

Gibs' eyes fall.

"…and Shannon got it! She totally got it. She was too real to go along with the program once she understood what phonies they were, but she loved them anyway, you know? She loved them and wanted them to be better, wanted our *family* to be better."

My eyes crinkle and unleash a fresh wave of tears.

"That's what your mom wants, too," Gibs says, intertwining his fingers.

"No!" My face turns jagged. "Mom doesn't want *better*. She wants *perfect*. But not real perfection, just her phony Christmas-card version of perfection."

"She wanted Shannon to be better," Gibs counters. "She was obviously worried about her. She tried to help her. I mean, she had her in counseling…"

"No, no, no!" I shake my head roughly. "She just wanted Shannon back to the way she used to be. She didn't want Shannon to understand her feelings, she wanted her to *deny* her feelings, to stop growing, to stop understanding, to stop seeing the family for what it really was. She wanted her perfect daughter back, but Shannon couldn't fake it anymore.

So she died feeling like a failure, just like I've felt every day of my life. And *Mom* is the failure, not us! Damn Mom. Damn her."

My sobs are whimpers now, and without thinking about it, I lay my head in Gibs' lap, my body curled into a ball. I feel his hand haltingly touch my hair. A few moments pass. I don't know exactly what I'm expecting Gibs to say, but God, I feel like I see things so clearly now, so I assume he's getting it.

"You say your mom's standards are too high," Gibs says, and I can already tell by his professorish tone that he's not getting it at all. "Well, your standards for *her* seem awfully high, if you ask me."

I stiffen. "What do you mean?"

"Jesus, Summer," he says. "Some mothers beat the crap out of their kids, or lock them in dark closets, or don't give them enough to eat, you know? A lot of kids really have it rough. Your mom ... sure, she has her issues, but she's a nice lady who's trying her best. She doesn't get the whole control-freak thing. It's just who she is. I mean, was it a crime for her to want Shannon to make A's in school or prefer that she stop sneaking out of the house to smoke pot with a loser boyfriend? You make Shannon sound like she was Gandhi, for Christ's sake."

I sit up, turn away from Gibs, and press my knees against my chest, staring out the window. It's begun raining, one of those schizoid sunshine-rainstorms. "You don't understand," I say coldly.

"I *do*," Gibs says. He takes my arms and tries to prod

me in his direction, but I don't budge. The rain is falling harder now.

He sighs, tosses his head backward, and squeezes the bridge of his nose. "Yeah, your *mom's* the ice princess," he mutters wearily.

I gasp a little, then stand up and face him. "I am *so* out of here."

"See?" he says, flinging his palms in my direction. "You expect your mom to see things in herself that *you* can't see in *your*self. Not so easy, huh? So why don't you give her a friggin' break, Summer? She's not the only one who has a hard time seeing things from anybody's perspective other than her own."

I'm frozen in place. I want to leave, but I'll be damned if I do anything to prove his point, whatever his point might be. So I just keep standing there, my jaw set and my eyes narrowed to slits. My gaze bores into his and I expect him to look away, but he doesn't. He just keeps looking back, but his eyes are soft.

"What am I not seeing?" I finally ask, trying to keep my voice steady.

He takes my hand and holds it loosely. "That you're a lot like your mom. And that's not such a bad thing."

Twenty-Five

"Gibs thinks I'm too hard on Mom."

Aunt Nicole's eyes stay focused on the bright-yellow button poms she's arranging in a vase. The screen door squeaks lazily. The first customer of the week has just come and gone, a fistful of peonies in her hand, and the flower shop is sighing and creaking in her wake as Aunt Nic resumes her flower-arranging.

"I'm just frustrated she hasn't changed," I continue, lightly fingering one of the velvety blossoms.

Aunt Nic tucks a sprig of baby's breath into the vase, then faces me, resting a hand on her hip. "How do you want her to change, honey?"

I surprise myself by feeling tears spring to my eyes. Aunt Nic's eyebrows weave anxiously and she guides me to the loveseat by the work table.

"It's weird," I say as we sit down. "I've always assumed *I* was the reason Mom was so uptight…because I was such a screw-up. I figured I made her a perfectionist because I was so unperfect."

"*Im*perfect," Aunt Nic says, winking at me playfully.

"Right. It's like, if you're allergic to peanuts, you may never even know it until you eat one. No peanuts, no problem." I search her face.

"I'm the peanut," I explain.

She smiles patiently. "I get it, sweetie."

"So I figured, Shannon was perfect, which made Mom perfectly happy. But now I see that Shannon wasn't perfect, and it made her crazy trying to pretend she was." I pick up a throw pillow and squeeze it against my chest. "Shannon kinda took the pressure off me, you know? I mean, I've known my whole life I could never be as great as her, so I didn't even try. But what if there hadn't been any Shannon? Then I would have felt all the pressure *she* had, with Mom expecting perfect looks, perfect grades, perfect blah-blah-blah-blah-*blah*."

I squeeze the pillow tighter. Aunt Nicole reaches over and runs her hand through my hair.

"And she was able to keep it up for a long time," I continue, peering into space. "She kept tap-dancing as long as she could for Mom until she was too exhausted to do it anymore. By that time, she was so furious at Mom, she couldn't see straight. Then, instead of being just a run-of-the-mill screw-up, like me, she had to make herself the *perfect* screw-up. She went nuts the last few months of her life, hanging out with some pothead girl, sneaking off nights with a loser boyfriend..."

"Mmmmm. I remember," Aunt Nic says in a sad, dreamy voice.

"I feel so sorry for her when I read her journal," I say, my shoulders tensing. "I want to go back in time, tell Mom to back off and tell Shannon she can relax and just be herself. I don't think she could ever *relax*. I love Mom, but she makes it so hard to relax."

I sigh, exhausted just at the thought.

"So," Nic says tentatively, "have you told your mother any of this?"

I shrug. "Bits and pieces, I guess. But she can't hear it. She couldn't hear it from Shannon and she can't hear it from me. It keeps us all stuck."

"But your mom was in counseling with Shannon those last few months," Aunt Nic says.

"That drove Shannon the craziest of all," I say in a pleading voice. "It's like the shrink gave her a glimpse of what it could be like to live as something other than Mom's trophy kid, and it gave her hope. But Mom didn't want any part of it. She just wanted the shrink to fix Shannon, like *Shannon* was the problem."

Aunt Nicole smiles wanly. "And where does your dad fit into all of this?" she asks. "I mean, he was her parent, too. Does he get any of the blame?"

I shake my head roughly. "I'm not blaming. I mean, I know it sounds like I am, but I'm not. I don't think Shannon was blaming anybody either, not really. I know she was on a total *screw you* kick for a while, but she loved Mom and wanted so much for her to love her back."

Aunt Nic's eyes flood with concern. "Oh, Summer, if I know nothing else, I know that your mom worshipped the ground Shannon walked on."

"She wanted Mom to love her *unconditionally*," I stress. "Mom can never quite manage that. I tried to talk to her yesterday, and she froze me out. Damn, I'm *still* feeling guilty about it." I shake my head slowly. "You know, you pay a huge price when you use guilt to get your way."

Aunt Nicole puts her palm against my cheek. "I'm so sorry, sweetie," she says, then lowers her voice to a whisper. "I think it was a mistake to give you that journal. I think this is way, way too hard for..."

"No!" I insist. "Hard is okay. *Sad* is okay. And mad is okay. I wish Shannon had known that. Shouldn't Mom have learned that? After everything she went through with Shannon, why is she still laying guilt trips on me?"

Aunt Nicole takes my hands. "She *did* learn, Summer. Maybe not enough, but she's different with you than she was with Shannon. Just look at you. You're so confident and independent. You don't care what other people think. You don't care about conforming. That came from somewhere, you know."

I laugh wryly. "Not from Mom. I'm that way in *spite* of her, not because of her. Why is Mom so rigid?"

Aunt Nicole smiles wryly. "You've met Grandma? You know, a little old gray-haired lady about yea high?"

I smile and nod knowingly.

"Yep, if genes have anything to do with personality, then your mom definitely comes by her rigidity honestly," she says. "Plus, our childhood was a little, um…challenging." Aunt Nic continues in a softer voice. "Nothing awful, but your grandpa drank too much, and he was in and out of jobs pretty regularly."

I glance at her, surprised.

She nods. "Grandpa's fine now. He's come a long way. But you know, sometimes you don't necessarily *want* to be a control freak, but life demands it of you. If Grandma hadn't been cracking the whip all those years, who knows how we might have ended up. She held everything together. And your mom, well, she was the oldest, so…"

"Mom never told me any of this," I say.

Aunt Nic lightly bites her lower lip. "There were plenty of times your mom was more like a mother to me than a sister. If Grandma was suddenly having to work an extra shift or take in laundry or whatever, your mom was the one who made sure I brushed my teeth and had clean clothes to wear to school the next morning. And it didn't bother me a bit. Sure, she was bossy, but knowing *somebody* was in control felt like the best thing in the world to me."

My hands clench. "I didn't even know Grandpa drank."

Aunt Nic sucks in her lips. "He hasn't had a drop in years. He stopped around the time we started high school. Grandma finally gave him an ultimatum, and I guess she convinced him she meant it." She pats my knee. "Things were better from then on, much better. But by that time, your mom's role was pretty entrenched."

I shake my head. "Why won't she tell me these things? I'd understand her so much better if she'd just be honest with me."

Aunt Nic squeezes my hand. "She didn't want her girls lugging around any of her baggage. She wanted your lives to be perfect."

My chin quivers. "Honest is better than perfect."

Aunt Nic nods smartly. "Right you are. And honesty has the damnedest way of asserting itself."

"I wish you could have said these things to Shannon," I say.

Aunt Nic gives me a guarded look. "Shannon wasn't nearly as mature as you are," she says. "I tried talking to her a few times, especially after she found out about her dad's affair, but she shut me out. She just wasn't ready to handle it."

"I guess shutting people out runs in the family," I say with a rueful laugh.

Aunt Nic puts an arm around my shoulder and I nestle my head into the crook of her neck. She fingers a lock of my hair as the scent of roses wafts through the air.

She hasn't uttered a word yet about the question I need answered the most: Does she know if Shannon committed suicide? Does she even suspect it?

And I'm not asking. I don't think I'm ready for the answer yet.

I take a deep breath and sigh, wishing I could reach back in time and guide my sister when she needed help the most.

Twenty-Six

I'm in the bathroom after work, wrapping my wet hair in a towel, when I hear my cell phone ringing.

I tighten the sash on my terrycloth robe, hurry into my bedroom, and grab my cell phone.

"Hello?"

"Hi, uh … Summer?"

"Yes, this is Summer."

"Oh. Gosh, you even sound like Shannon."

My grip on the phone tightens.

"This is Eve. Shannon's friend from high school."

My mouth drops open and I stand frozen in space for a moment.

"Oh … hi." I shut my bedroom door, then walk over to my bed and sit down. When I finally got up the nerve to call her last night, I got her answering machine. Frankly,

I was relieved. What would I have said to her if she'd answered? How do you just barge into someone's life, mutter a few pleasantries, and then begin barking out personal questions about the past? I guess I'm about to find out.

"Thanks for calling me back," I say.

"Sure." Her voice is soft and kind, like her mom's.

Awkward silence.

"Um..." I say, then realize I need to get to the point. "Eve, my sister kept a journal the summer before she died."

"Oh..."

"I didn't know about it until a few weeks ago. My aunt had been holding on to it, and she gave it to me on—"

"Summer, I'm so sorry I haven't kept in touch with your family," Eve blurts out, sounding like she's on the verge of tears.

"It's okay..."

"No, it's not," Eve says. "Shannon was my best friend. Your mother was like my second mom. I sent her cards for a few years, but I never really knew what to say, and—"

"Really, Eve, it's okay. That's not why I'm—"

"But I need to say it. And I need to say it to your mother. In person. I'm flying in to visit my mom in early August. Do you think we could come by? If it would upset your mother, just tell me. But I want to let her know I've never stopped thinking about Shannon. Or her."

I straighten up, a little impatient. This phone call was supposed to be about what *I* need. But how stupid does that sound? As if the people in Shannon's life are characters in a book. Props. That's how they feel when I read her journal. I blush with shame.

"Sure, you can come by," I tell Eve. "I know my mom would love to see you. But I'm reading some things in Shannon's journal that I don't think my mom knew about. Can I ask you about some of those things?"

Pause. Then, warily: "Yes."

"I know you and Shannon had grown apart toward the end," I say.

"And I'm so sorry about that, too," Eve gushes.

"It's okay," I say firmly. "I didn't say it to make you feel bad. I just said it because I'm not sure how much you knew about the last few months of her life."

Another pause. "I knew," Eve says.

"You knew she was sneaking out to see Chris?"

"Yes. I hated him, and Shannon thought it was because I was . . . I don't know . . . jealous or something. Neither of us had dated much in high school. Every guy in school was in love with Shannon, but I guess she seemed like she was out of their league, so they were too scared to approach her. Me, I was just awkward and nerdy."

I laugh nervously.

"Anyway, when Chris started flirting with Shannon, she really fell hard," Eve continues. "I told her I thought he was bad news, but she didn't want to hear it. Then she started hanging around this girl named Jamie."

"Were you and Jamie friends, too?"

"No." Even over the phone, I can hear the distaste in Eve's voice.

"Were Shannon and Chris still together when she died?"
I ask.

Pause.

I'm confused. Maybe Eve didn't hear my question.
"Were Shannon and Chris...?"

"I don't know. There were some rumors..."

I swallow. "What kind of rumors?"

"Just...just that Chris was...seeing other girls behind
her back."

I swallow. "Her journal makes it sound like he did
everything short of stamping *cheater* on his forehead. But
she kept defending him."

"She was just so in love," Eve says. "I understand that.
He was really cute. She was ready for something different,
and he was...different."

I lightly tap my index finger against the phone. "She
missed you," I say. "I mean, she wrote about you a lot in
her journal, even though you didn't see much of each other
that summer."

Pause. "She wrote about me?" Eve asks, her voice catching.

"Yeah. Sounds like you two had a great friendship."

Eve sniffs on the other end of the phone.

"She really cared about you," I say. "She knew you were
a true friend. She was just...dealing with a lot of stuff."

"I know," Eve says.

Another awkward pause.

"Did you know she was seeing a psychologist?" I ask.

"No," Eve says, sounding genuinely surprised. "But

I'm glad. She had a lot of things to sort out." She clears her throat.

"Do you think you would have gotten close again if she hadn't—"

"Oh, I know we would have. We were like sisters. And we had all these plans. We were going to room together in college. Then join the Peace Corps!"

I press my lips together tightly.

Eve clears her throat again. "Anyway, those last few months...they were an aberration. I knew Shannon would come around. Actually, we went shopping with our mothers just a few days before...just before she...before she passed away. We talked and cried and hugged. *She* was sorry, *I* was sorry, it was all water under the bridge. We couldn't wait for our senior year to start."

My heart skips a beat. Eve makes Shannon sound so hopeful, so optimistic. But Eve didn't know everything; it's toward the very end of the journal that Shannon wrote, *I want to kill myself.* If it *was* suicide, Eve is totally clueless.

That's a good sign...right?

Eve sniffles some more. "That's the last time I saw her, the last time I talked to her. I miss her so much."

I bite my lower lip to steady the quiver in my chin.

I miss her, too.

Twenty-Seven

B...*R*...*A*...*T. Bratworst.*"

I yelp with joy. It was sheer genius to build on the word *worst*. This is my best Scrabble round ever.

Gibs and his parents exchange glances.

My eyes dart from one face to the next. "What?" I demand.

"Bratwurst is spelled with a *U*," his dad says apologetically. "*W-U*. Not *W-O*."

My jaw drops. "You are so kidding."

They shake their heads. "But I can check the dictionary, if you want," Gibs says.

I hold up the palm of my hand, then scoop up my now-useless *B*, *R*, *A*, and *T* tiles. "No, I get that you're all freakishly brilliant and happen to know that off the top of your heads," I mutter playfully.

I peer at my tiles to reconsider my options, then reluctantly add an *E* to the bottom of the *W* in *worst*, giving an exaggerated sigh.

"*We* is a perfectly good word," Gibs' mom says, and we laugh at her earnestness.

I inhale deeply, savoring the salty scent of the ocean breeze mixing with the aroma of the boiled shrimp we had for dinner an hour earlier.

The past four days have been incredible, swimming with Gibs in the surf, paddling a kayak, collecting shells on the shore, watching campy movies on an overstuffed sofa at two a.m., seeing fireworks on the beach on the Fourth of July, jogging with him and his parents on the sand, and now losing badly at Scrabble after dinner on the deck of the beach house. As much fun as we've had, I'm pretty clear at this point that I'm firmly affixed in Gibs' "friend" box. Whatever I was expecting to happen that might nudge us into the couples category isn't happening. But you know what? I'm okay with that. I'll take Gibs as a friend over any other guy on the planet as a boyfriend.

It's Gibs' turn at Scrabble, and he scratches his head as he studies his tiles. A few seconds later, he adds *D, E, L,* and *N* to my *We*. I stare at him incredulously.

"*We-deln?*" I say.

"It's a skiing term," he responds. "It's pronounced *VAHD-lyn*."

The family resumes their glance-exchanging.

"I surrender!" I moan, burying my face in my hands. "My ego won't survive another turn."

"Good," Gibs says, standing up from his spot on the floor. "I'd rather walk on the beach than play Scrabble anyhow."

His parents and I look out toward the ocean.

"Aaaahh. The sun is setting," his mom says, pulling a lock of dark, curly hair behind her ear.

"So ... anyone care to join me?"

"Sure," his mom and I say simultaneously.

"Um ... on second thought," she adds, "maybe Dad and I will stay and finish the game."

I rise to my feet and wipe my hands on the back of my shorts. "Sorry I won't be here to help you with your spelling," I say.

They laugh lightly as Gibs and I head down the cedar steps leading from the deck to the beach.

I'm accustomed to Gibs' extra-long strides by now, so I trot a little to keep up once our feet hit the sand. His arms swing as he saunters closer to the water. His ponytail, curlier than usual in the ocean air, bounces with every step.

"Trying to keep up with you is like trying to keep up with a greyhound," I say from a few steps behind, tightening my own ponytail as it blows in the breeze.

He turns around with a smile and extends his hand. I eye it tentatively, then grab hold. I yelp as he pulls me closer, then loosen my grip so our fingers can fall apart.

Except that they don't. Because Gibs is still squeezing my hand.

He peers out at the horizon as we walk in the surf. The waves slosh against our ankles.

"Look," I say, pointing at a water skier with my free hand. "A we-deln."

He laughs. "*VAHD-lyn*. It's pronounced *VAHD-lyn*. But that guy isn't one. VAHD-lyn is a snow-skiing term. And it doesn't describe the skier, it describes a style of skiing."

I stick my tongue out at him. He's still holding my hand.

"Who knows this kind of stuff?" I ask him, and he shrugs.

"Tell me something you don't know," I challenge him.

He peers skyward. "Hmmmm … can't do it. Apparently I know everything."

I splash him with my foot. My hand is starting to feel comfortable in his.

"I mean it," I persist. "Tell me something you don't know."

He squints at me, then looks back toward the ocean. "I don't know lots of things."

"Such as?"

"Such as … Britney Spears' middle name."

"Oooh, me, me!" I say, raising my free hand. "I know it. It's Jean."

"Well, there you have it," Gibs says. "I know the definition of *wedeln* and you know Britney Spears' middle name. There's symmetry in the world after all."

"More," I say, breaking into a skip. "Tell me something else you don't know and we'll see if I know it."

His eyebrows knit together. "How to make beef stroganoff?"

I wince. "I could do it with Hamburger Helper. Does that count?"

"Works for me."

Still holding hands.

Gibs stops abruptly, finally letting go of my hand. He turns to face me but doesn't make eye contact. "Here's something I don't know," he says, digging his toe into the wet sand.

Long pause.

"Yeah?" I prod.

A wave splashes over our feet.

He rubs his hands together. "I don't know how to tell a girl I love her."

Longer pause.

"Especially," he continues, "when we have two more potentially very awkward days to be at the beach together."

I search his eyes, but he won't look at me. Oh, God. He *is* there, after all.

I laugh at his awkwardness. "No way," I say, still not sure I'm clear on this extremely cool turn of events.

He shrugs. "Way."

"So ... I'm the girl?"

"Uh, check."

I nod appreciatively. "Dude. That was much more romantic than I would've given you credit for."

I figure glibness is the best way to override my impulse to leap in the air and throw myself into my arms.

He presses his lips together, still staring at the sand. "Why do I feel like I'm being graded?"

I giggle at him again. "Hey, no problem. You definitely rate an A."

His dark blue eyes flicker in my direction, then dart away again.

I stroke my chin thoughtfully. "Just to make sure I've got this straight: You, like, *love* me."

Gibs stuffs his hands in the pockets of his blue jean shorts, squeezes his eyes shut, and shakes his head slowly. "I am such an idiot," he mutters.

"*In* love," I clarify.

Gibs plops down on the sand and covers his face with his hands. I sit beside him and pull his hands away. "It's okay. I dig you, too. I just didn't think you were there yet."

A breeze blows his ponytail as he looks me in the eye. "I'm right here," he says.

Then he kisses me.

Our last two days at the beach are decidedly low-key. Neither Gibs nor I are much for public displays of affection anyway, and God knows we don't want to give his parents any fodder for talking about what an adorable couple we are. So we stick with the program: Scrabble, late-night movies on the sofa, body-surfing in the waves … the same stuff we've done all week long.

But God, that kiss.

His salty lips were so soft and moist. The way he cupped his hand around my face was so intimate. The way he held my face close after we'd kissed and just kept staring at my mouth, like he'd stumbled onto the Holy Grail … God, it was intense.

Why does this seem so natural? Shouldn't it take more than one kiss to shed a year's worth of just-friends vibes? Shouldn't we be throat-clearing, eye-averting, stammering messes as we deal with the awkwardness of it all?

Except that it isn't awkward. One minute, he was my friend, and the next, he's kissing me.

And it just feels right.

We're packing up to go home, and Gibs' parents have walked to the car with the first batches of luggage. Gibs and I are in the kitchen, me with my head in the cupboard as I hand him leftover groceries that he stacks in a box. From my peripheral vision, I notice him doing a double take after his parents leave to make sure they're out the door. He spins around and grabs me around the waist.

I squeal, turn to face him, then melt into a kiss.

It's another perfect kiss, long and slow and moist and soft. We pull apart with my arms still around the back of his neck, his still around my waist.

"So … you wanna get married?" I ask him, and we laugh.

"I've spent months kissing you in my head," he says.

No way. Me, too. "Kissing me on my face has got to be a step up."

"Oh, yeah." He kisses me again.

"Jeez, Gibs," I tease. "I'm thinking you wanna be my boyfriend or something."

He wrinkles his nose and smiles at me. "Okay."

I bite my lip. "Can we do that? The whole boyfriend-girlfriend thing?"

He nods. "Yeah, I'm thinking we can."

I giggle at him. "I don't know, Gibs. Corsages might be involved. Long, sucky notes in each other's yearbooks, Facebook photos of us staring into each other's eyes... things like that."

He peers into space as he thinks about it, still holding me in his arms. "I'm good with that," he finally announces.

I sputter with laughter. "You *so* are not."

"I so am!" he protests playfully, then squints his eyes sheepishly. "Okay, maybe the Facebook photos would be a stretch. I just want to be with you. And I definitely want to kiss you some more. A lot more, actually."

We lean in to kiss again, but we hear the front door open and hastily pull apart. But our eyes are still locked together.

Here's the thing about Gibs' eyes: they look like shimmery ponds at midnight that I could skinny-dip in without getting cold or wet. I'd just float in silky warmth.

"Got those groceries packed?" his mother asks cheerfully.

Right. The groceries.

Twenty-Eight

"Hi, Shannon."

I smile sleepily as I finger the journal I've retrieved from under my mattress.

I feel a little disloyal. I've gone days without touching it, and truthfully, I didn't even give it much thought at the beach. Is it okay for Gibs to trump Shannon? I don't know. I'm still trying to figure out where she fits in my life.

Anyway, now that I'm back, I'm eager to reconnect with her. I'm exhausted from the long ride home, and even after a shower, I still have a little sand between my toes that I'll have to rinse off in the morning before I go to work. And God, I can barely hold my eyes open, and even with my eyes open, it's hard to think about anything but Gibs and those moist, salty kisses. But still . . . I want to touch base with my sister.

I wish I could tell Shannon about Gibs. I wonder if she'd like him. Would she think we make a good couple? Would she approve of my decision to utter not a word to Mom, lest she start picking out china patterns? And speaking of boyfriends—has she finally had enough sense to dump that loser, Chris?

I open the journal.

Monday, July 5, 1993

What a difference a day makes.

   Yesterday, I was on top of the world. I spent the day at the lake with Chris, Jamie, and some other people, sunbathing and swimming all day, then shooting fireworks that night. Chris and I necked under the stars. Oooooohh, I love him so much. And I don't care what Dr. Deadhead says, he loves me, too, and I know our future together is as bright as the neon fireworks that emblazoned the sky as we kissed.

Oh, God. Please tell me I'll never be lovesick enough to sound that sappy. It's journal entries like these that make me think I never would have been friends with Shannon in high school. How can she be so awesome, and then be so juvenile? I keep reading:

   Speaking of Dr. Deadhead, thank God his office was closed today, because otherwise I'd be tempted to tell him what happened this morning. (I tease him that he's like a Russian spy: He has "vays" of making me talk.)

Jamie spent the night after we got back from the lake (I sneaked her in so Mom wouldn't freak), then we went to the mall first thing this morning so I could get home in time for my 1 p.m. shift at the pool.

Anyhow, we were just killing time, browsing in the stores, when Jamie started trying to twist my arm to buy her some perfume.

I said no, and this time I meant it. I work too hard, baking in the hundred-degree sun, to spend my paycheck on her. When I think of all the jeans and shirts and earrings she's talked me into buying her—God, I'm such a sap. Besides, it's not like she appreciates anything. As soon as I buy her one thing, she's begging for something else.

I never mentioned this little tidbit to Dr. Deadhead, but I know what he'd say, and of course he'd be right.

So this time, I didn't let her wear me down. "No," I told her, just like I'd tell a two-year-old she couldn't have another cookie. "No, no, no." When it finally sank in that I meant it, what did she do?

You guessed it—she slipped a bottle of perfume in her purse and waltzed out the door like she owned the place. She said that's the trick to shoplifting— hold your head high and practically DARE some minimum-wage sales clerk to look your way.

I almost died, begging her to take the perfume back. She just laughed at me. Leave it to Jamie to make me feel hopelessly lame for having issues with stealing.

Even worse, we ran into Mr. Kibbits right outside the store, and I've never felt so guilty in my life. He was so great, giving us both a hug and wanting to know all about our summer. I stood there stammering my head off and shaking like a leaf.

Jamie, of course, was cool as a cucumber. She even took the perfume out of her purse and spritzed herself while we were talking to him! I thought my heart was going to explode.

She doubled over laughing when Mr. Kibbits finally walked away, telling me I looked like a bomb was strapped to my ankle.

That used to kinda work on me, Jamie acting so cool and funny about whatever stupid thing she was doing that I'd lighten up and figure it was no big deal.

Those days are history.

Yes, I still love Jamie, and I really think I'm a good influence on her (God, such a Mom thing to say), but seriously, all the stuff that used to seem so cool is now seeming pretty uncool. Or worse, felonious.

So I wouldn't speak to her for the next fifteen minutes, but then SHE had the nerve to get mad at ME. She walked away and I figured she'd come right back, but she never did. She left me stranded right there at the mall! Can you believe it? The ONE time she actually drives us some place, she ditches me!

Thank heaven I caught up with Mr. Kibbits and gave him some lame excuse for needing a ride home.

He gave me a little heart-to-heart on the way home about trusting the right people and not letting people take advantage of you, so he must have suspected what was up, or at least had a pretty good idea that if Jamie was involved, some kind of trouble was brewing. And what could I say? I couldn't even look him in the eye.

Anyhow, have I gotten so much as ONE CALL since then from Jamie checking up on me and making sure I'm okay? I could have been butchered by a serial murderer for all she knows. NOT ONE CALL!

I tried pouring my heart out to Chris, but he and his dad are busy tonight with a transmission or whatever, so here I am, lying in my bed and writing in my journal.

Jamie's supposed to come hang out at the pool tomorrow during my shift and I'm sure she won't even mention what happened. That's her. She says when something's over, it's over. Move on.

Easy for her to say. She's not the one who had to find a ride home from the mall.

I lay the journal on my chest. Jeez, I just want to throttle Shannon right now. It's one thing to rebel against Mom and Dad, but it's another to be a total idiot.

Damn. I was so tired when I picked up the journal,

and now my adrenaline's flowing and making me restless. I pick the journal back up.

Monday, July 12, 1993

I think Dr. Deadhead finally gets it.

He convinced me to let Mom and Dad sit in on my session today, and we might as well have been his guests at the opera.

As in sitting quietly, being polite and saying NOTHING. It was excruciating.

Poor Dr. Deadhead is used to me blathering on a mile a minute, but I was totally tongue-tied with Mom and Dad in the room.

Mom spent a few minutes doing her little spiel about what a fabulous family we are, very well-connected in the community, personal friends with the MAYOR, don't you know, had him over for dinner just last week as a matter of fact, blah blah blah blah BLAH.

When Dr. Deadhead commented that "appearances seem very important" to Mom, she got all tense and defensive, saying there's nothing fake or phony about her life, and is it a crime to be a stellar citizen and have the mayor over for dinner, and she certainly didn't mean to come across as BOASTFUL, she just thought Dr. Deadhead wanted to understand our lives, and really she's the most unpretentious, down-to-earth gal you'll ever want to meet, and oh by the way, is Shannon cured of her little rebellious phase yet?

Dr. Deadhead was Mister Diplomacy, saying OF COURSE we're a stellar little family, and kudos on the whole mayor deal, but maybe, just maybe, a little too much energy goes into trying to make things look great to the outside world without addressing problems under our own roof.

Ouch.

He didn't mention specifics, just danced around "ways that family members might try to get their needs met if they think their feelings are unacceptable," and Mom assured him that she accepts ALL our feelings, our family is like a feeling factory, she's all about feelings, and oh by the way, is Shannon cured of her little rebellious phase yet?

When Dr. Deadhead asked Mom about her own childhood, she got on a soapbox about how, no offense, but psychobabble gets on her nerves, and what possible relevance could her childhood have on my "issues" anyway, and oh by the way, is Shannon cured of her little rebellious phase yet?

Dr. Deadhead said he understood how Mom felt, but that if we were willing to shine a little light on issues that make us uncomfortable, those issues will be more manageable, and isn't that a good thing?

But Mom never budged from her defense post, and Dad never said much of anything. But when

Dr. Deadhead said he just wanted to help me feel happier, it's Dad who got teary-eyed.

So that's how it went in Dr. Deadhead's office today. At dinner tonight, Mom said in a snotty tone, "Well, he certainly has US pegged."

She thought she was being sarcastic.

I close the journal and hug it against my chest. *It's Dad who got teary-eyed.* I wonder if I've been selling him short. Maybe he can go deeper than I've given him credit for. I mean, he was willing to sit in a shrink's office, for Christ's sake. Who could have imagined that?

Then I get it: anything for Shannon. He was willing to do anything for Shannon, including breaking up with Church Slut and moving back into Mom's igloo. I feel a little stab in my heart. God, he loved Shannon so much. Why do I feel jealous? It's ridiculous. I mean, he's here for me, after all, just like he was for her. But he's just going through the motions now. Sure, he loves me, blah, blah, blah, but Shannon was the one who could bring him to tears.

On the other hand, maybe if *I* could loosen up a little, could let myself be a little vulnerable, could crack the door open just a tad, then maybe...

Maybe Dad would be willing to do anything for me, too.

Twenty-Nine

"What's it like to have a functional family?"

The merry-go-round squeaks lazily as a hot summer breeze nudges us into the slightest of motion.

The day after we got back from the beach, Gibs left for a second Habitat for Humanity project and suggested a picnic at the park for today, his first day back. God, I've missed him. We're sitting on a rusty merry-go-round eating grapes and PB&Js from paper sacks on my lunch hour. Kids are flitting around us on swings and slides as their moms watch from benches and slap mosquitoes off their arms.

"Functional?" Gibs asks.

"Yeah. As opposed to *dys*functional. It's just so clear, in Shannon's journal, how hopelessly screwed up my family is. All this denial, all this pretense ... just a mess, you know?"

Gibs shrugs. "Every family's got their stuff to deal with."

I shake my head. "Not yours. Your parents are great. They're so smart and funny. And real."

"As opposed to your imaginary parents."

Some smart-aleck skinny kid runs up and pushes one of our merry-go-round bars, darting away before we can object.

Actually, he did us a favor. The breeze feels nice.

"You know what I mean," I say. "You can talk to your parents. They really listen to you. They accept you for who you are. What the hell must *that* be like?"

Gibs pops a grape in his mouth. "We have our issues."

"Name one," I challenge him. "Name a Brown Family issue."

He peers thoughtfully into the slate-blue sky. "My mom's depression-prone."

I swallow hard. I didn't expect a real issue.

"Really?" I ask.

He nods, still looking past me. "She deals with it, but it can be a bitch."

I bounce a few words around in my head before I ask my next question. "Is she on medication or anything?"

"She's tried a few things, but she only takes drugs as a last resort. Mostly she's into exercise and diet, staying busy, writing in her journal ..."

"She keeps a journal, too?"

Gibs nods. "She's a really good writer. I think the flip

side to her gifts is that all that creativity and empathy make her hyper-attuned to *every*thing. She can never just chill. She just feels things really deeply. I'm sad that things weigh so heavily on her, but at the same time, it's such a basic part of who she is."

I wrap my fingers loosely around a rusty bar. "I didn't know. She doesn't *seem* depressed."

Gibs eats another grape. "She's usually fine. Even when she isn't so fine, she copes. I think that's what most people do, at least the ones who manage to hang on—they deal with their crap and find ways to keep going."

He sticks the heel of his shoe in the sandy dirt, grinding our merry-go-round to a halt.

"This thing makes me dizzy," he says.

I laugh at him, a little relieved that he's changed the subject. "You're the one who talked me into parasailing at the beach, but you can't handle a merry-go-round?"

He grins with his lips squeezed shut, which is when his dimple becomes most prominent.

"You're kinda adorable," I tell him, leaning closer.

He leans in, too, and we kiss underneath the rusty bar as our fingers intertwine around it.

"Summer? Gibson?"

Gibs and I glance up, alarmed. We squint into the sunlight and see Leah Rollins and Kendall Popwell.

"Hi," I say, offering a little wave with one hand while I shield my eyes with the other. "What are you two doing here?"

"Cheerleading practice," Leah says, tilting her head in

the direction of the recreation center a few hundred feet away. She looks at us quizzically. "So you two are a couple?"

"This is, like, breaking news?" I ask playfully.

"Uh, duh," Leah says, but her smile is friendly. "If you two Facebooked like normal people, we could keep up with these things."

I smile back. "Well, consider yourself informed."

Leah turns to Gibs. "Have you dug all the splinters out of your hands yet?"

I glance at him quizzically.

"I'm getting there," he says congenially.

"And blisters!" Leah says, holding up her hands for inspection. "I must have a dozen blisters!"

Gibs smiles, still shielding his eyes against the sun.

"Blisters from what?" Kendall asks.

Yeah. That's what I'd like to know.

"Habitat," Leah responds. "Gibs and I did a Habitat for Humanity project over the weekend. Part of our IB volunteer work."

My eyebrows furrow as I search Gibs' face for a reaction. There is none.

"Gloves," he tells Leah simply. "You gotta wear work gloves when you're hammering."

"*Now* you tell me."

They keep chatting for a couple more minutes, but the thud in my stomach has churned its way up my neck. I can feel blood pounding against my ears.

"Summer?"

I blink hard. "What?"

"I just asked if you're still working at your aunt's flower shop," Leah says.

"What? Oh, yeah."

"Mmmmm. Well, hey, it was great to see you two. Better get to practice," Leah says.

"Gloves," Gibs calls after her as she and Kendall start to walk away. "Don't forget your work gloves next time."

They laugh lightly.

My gaze bores into Gibs after the girls are out of earshot.

He doesn't notice at first, but then his eyes flicker toward mine, look away, turn back. "*What?*" he asks.

"Leah was with you on the Habitat for Humanity project?"

He looks confused. "*With* me?"

"Yes," I say in a steely voice.

"She was *there*," he clarifies. "She wasn't *with* me."

"Why?" I demand, feeling incredibly petty even as I say it but not being able to stop myself. A new knot is churning in my stomach. "Why was she there?"

"*Why?*" Gibs repeats, looking truly baffled. "Like I have any control over who volunteers for Habitat?"

"You have control over whether you tell me," I say, my chin quivering.

He squeezes his eyes shut and then pops them open. "Why would I tell you that? Why would you care? Do you want to know the other forty volunteers who were there, too? A roster of names, maybe?"

"Not a word," I mutter bitterly. "You didn't say **one** word to me about it."

His hands fly in the air. "Okay. *A*—this is the first time I've seen you since I got back, and *B*—since when have you asked me one word about my volunteer work?"

"I've asked!" I protest.

Gibs rolls his eyes. "I barely got a word in edgewise after my first Habitat trip. Since when have you cared? Let's face it, *my* activities haven't exactly been our main topic of conversation lately. It's not so easy competing with Shannon."

I hide my face in my hands, jump off the merry-go-round, and start running, peering through splayed fingers.

"Summer!"

I hear Gibs sprinting behind me, so I run faster.

"Summer!"

I reach my car in the parking lot, jump in, and slam the door. Gibs is running toward me, his arms pumping and his sneakers pounding the pavement.

My tires squeal as I back out of the parking space and tear out of the parking lot.

Gibs stands in a cloud of fumes, getting smaller and smaller in my rearview mirror as I drive away.

———

I can barely see through a blur of tears as I screech away from the park.

Slow down, you idiot. You want Mom and Dad to lose

two kids in car wrecks? And quit taking out your frustration on poor Gibs. You know who you need to deal with. Just grow up and do it.

I brush a tear off my cheek and ease off the accelerator. *Is that you, Shannon?* God, this is so ridiculous. I've never been spiritual before, but she feels kinda... *here.* What's more, it's a good feeling. Shannon makes me feel like someone's in my corner. Even if she's slapping me silly trying to cram some sense into my thick head.

I glance at the clock on my dashboard. I'd planned to spend my whole lunch hour with Gibs, but my little diva moment took care of that. I'm not due to be back at Aunt Nic's shop for another thirty-five minutes. I have time...

You know who you need to deal with. Just grow up and do it.

I take a deep breath, make a quick left, and head to Dad's office.

———

"Honey... hi."

Dad was so engrossed in his computer that it's taken him a couple seconds to realize I'm standing in his office. He gets up when he sees me and straightens his tie.

I wave self-consciously. I've been in Dad's office plenty of times, but I can't remember ever showing up unannounced.

"Sorry to just drop by..."

"Is anything wrong?" he asks, a touch of urgency in his voice.

"No, no…"

His face relaxes and he extends an arm toward a chair.

I sit down and breathe in the familiar leather scent. This is where I used to sit drinking vanilla Cokes when I was little, watching Dad type on his computer or issue calm, precise directions on the phone, surrounded by framed school photos of Shannon and me.

Tension weaves back into Dad's face. "You've been crying," he says.

I blush a little, but I'm touched he noticed.

"What is it?" Dad asks, leaning into his desk.

I glance toward the door to make sure I remembered to close it. I can hear voices outside Dad's office, but just barely. We have plenty of privacy.

I tap my fingertips together. "Dad, I'm sorry to just show up and spring this on you, but I was afraid if I waited until later, I'd lose my nerve…"

His face stays totally calm, but whatever he's holding in his hands snaps in two. I look closer: a pencil. The sound made me jump.

"Honey, are you okay?" he asks evenly, his jaw firm.

"Yes, yes. I'm fine. I just… found something out." My eyes sneak a glance at his, but I quickly look away. *Just say it, Summer.* "I found out about your affair."

The next few seconds hang in the air like kudzu, thick and suffocating.

His brown eyes flood with regret. "I'm so sorry, honey,"

he says, in barely a whisper. "It was years ago, and it didn't mean anything..."

I shake my head. "It's okay, it's okay. I'm not telling you to make you feel bad." I hate seeing him look so sad.

"Aunt Nic?" Dad asks softly, and I shrug noncommittally. I guess technically, yeah, I *did* find out from Aunt Nic, and I don't think Dad could handle pulling Shannon into this conversation.

I don't know what I expect Dad to do. Shrivel into a fetal position? Start pounding his fists against his chest? But he sits up straighter. "Ask me anything," he says.

I sit there mutely. I have a million questions, yet I can't think of anything to say.

"It meant *nothing*," Dad repeats. "I was a stupid fool. I'll never forgive myself for putting my family through that. And I'll never do it again."

I swallow hard and blink away the tears that have suddenly formed in my eyes because...because I believe him. It feels so good to believe him.

"I know Mom's hard to live with..." I say, my voice breaking.

"Your mother is the strongest person I know," Dad says firmly.

I open my mouth to speak, but Dad's not finished yet.

"I know I haven't done a good job of letting you know how I feel about your mother. I guess I put my energy into trying to do the right thing—making a living, being home for dinner every day, helping around the house. But

I should say it out loud, how much I love her." His eyes mist. "I should say that to both of you more often."

I try to talk, but my voice catches. I clear my throat and start again. "I know that, Dad. I love you, too."

Dad's eyebrows weave together. "The irony is that adultery is what wrecked *my* childhood. I swore I would never do that to my family."

I eye him warily. I never knew his dad—he died before I was born—but I always assumed that he and Grandma Stetson were happily married.

"Your grandfather had several affairs," Dad says, loosening his tie as his face reddens. "It was awful for my mother. For all of us. I grew up feeling like I had to keep an eye on her every minute, make sure she was okay. She was depression-prone anyway, and the affairs... they really did a number on her."

Wow. All this information, right there at my fingertips. Why haven't my parents ever told me before? Why haven't I asked? *My family never talks about anything that matters...*

"Grandma Stetson always seems great to me," I say, picturing her playing bridge in Arizona and tooling around in a golf cart with her girlfriends.

"She's fine," Dad emphasizes. "But when my father was living, particularly when I was a little boy, there was always a lot of... turmoil."

I gaze out Dad's window, the afternoon glare just starting to pierce through his blinds. "Do all guys cheat?" I ask, my eyes tearing again.

Dad leans closer. "No. *No.*"

I start weeping, and he walks over and hugs me. It feels stiff and awkward at first—me burrowing deeper into the leather chair as his long arms reach toward me tentatively—but then I stand up and hug him back.

His embrace is so tight, it takes my breath away. But after I hug him back, we both exhale and relax. We stand there for a long time, just holding each other.

Thirty

*Y*ou're sure."

It's a question, not a statement. I smile wanly at Aunt Nic. "Yes. I'm sure."

I've been pretty preoccupied since I got back from my lunch hour. It's almost five, and this is the fifth time Aunt Nic has asked me if I'm okay. I guess subtlety isn't my strong suit.

"Why don't you go on home? I'll close up," she says.

"I don't mind staying." What else do I have to do?

She places her hands on my shoulders. "I'll close up. Go."

I smile appreciatively, go to the back of the store to get my purse, then wave as I walk out the front door, the bell jangling behind me.

How stupid of me to have expected Gibs to come to the flower shop, daisies in hand...

I get into my car and sit there for a second. I drop my head on the steering wheel and start to cry.

God, I'm tired of crying. And let me make this perfectly clear—I used to go weeks at a time, months even, without crying. Shannon's done such a number on me.

I jump, startled, as I hear a tap on my window. I look out and see Gibs, his eyes so sweet and kind. I motion for him to come around to the passenger side.

He climbs into the car, reaches over, and holds me tight.

"I'm sorry," he says in my ear.

I shake my head vigorously. "*I'm* sorry. Oh, God, Gibs, we've been together for all of two weeks and I've turned into a psycho girlfriend."

He smiles at me as we pull away from our embrace.

My eyebrows furrow. "I don't want to be my mom. I don't want to be an ice princess. And God knows I don't want to be some ridiculous, clingy, insecure flake. You deserve better. Maybe I'm not ready for this."

Gibs presses a finger lightly against my lips. "No names, no labels, no psychoanalysis, okay? People argue. People piss each other off. Stop being so hard on yourself."

My eyes search his. "If it had been anybody other than Leah Rollins..."

He laughs at my earnest expression, and I laugh back.

"She, like, totally stole my boyfriend in ninth grade, you know," I say, in my best Valley Girl impression.

He smiles, but then turns somber. "I don't care about Leah Rollins. I care about *you*."

I swallow hard, squinting through tear-stained eyes. "I'm sorry I've been so self-absorbed all summer. It's just...some of the stuff I've found out, about my dad, all this secret-keeping..."

"I won't keep secrets from you," Gibs says firmly. "I promise."

My fingers interlock with his. "Me too."

"Have faith in us, okay?" he says. "Let's not run away when we hit a rough patch. Let's work through it."

I nod. "That's the trick?"

He shakes his head. "No tricks. *That's* the trick."

I bite my lip. "You want me to shut up about Shannon?"

He shakes his head. "I want to share everything with you."

I take a deep breath. "I went to my dad's office after I left the park. I told him I knew about the affair."

Gibs nods, prodding me along.

"He told me that his dad cheated on his mother...that he hated him for it. He hates himself for doing the same thing to his family."

Gibs nods again. "Good," he says softly. "I'm glad you had that talk with your dad."

"Me, too. It's like Shannon is nudging us all out of our comfort zones. But I'm more comfortable outside my comfort zone than I thought I'd be."

Gibs smiles at me.

"I'm almost done, you know," I tell him. "With her journal, I mean. Then we can talk about … I don't know … drywall or calluses or whatever."

He drops his head and laughs.

"I'm interested. I really am," I say.

"You so are not," he says, stifling a laugh.

"Okay. I'm not. But I'll fake it for you."

"No faking, remember? Come with me next time we build a house and you'll see for yourself how cool it is."

"Will you bring me a pair of work gloves?"

"Yes. I'll bring the gloves."

"Well, then." I offer him my hand and he shakes it. "It's official."

———

I read another entry before I fall asleep.

Monday, July 19, 1993

I told Dr. Deadhead that I hated to tell him I told him so, but I told him so.

He said yeah, my parents are pretty tough nuts to crack. But he expected that, and he was paying more attention to ME while they were in the room than he was to THEM.

Why didn't I cry, he wondered, when my dad started crying in his office? I mean, how often do I see my dad cry? Like, maybe once in a blue moon? So wasn't it pretty intense to see my dad crying?

Uh, duh. But am I suddenly some kind of uncaring freak because it didn't make me cry to see him cry? And suddenly I realized, YES, that's exactly what I am—and THAT made me cry. So here I was bawling my eyes out in Dr. Deadhead's office because I DIDN'T cry when apparently I should have. It kills me to not do what I'm supposed to do. I guess I said that out loud to Dr. Deadhead, because he repeated it: It kills you?

Yes, I told him, yes yes yes yes yes, I can't bear letting people down. I'd rather die than let people down.

I lay the journal down as my heart quickens. *I want to kill myself.*

I swallow hard and pick it back up again.

Then Dr. Deadhead stopped taking notes and looked at me really carefully. "Do you ever think about hurting yourself?" he asked.

And I thought about that for a long time, because especially now that I know how closely he pays attention to me, I really want to give the right answer, and I guessed the right answer was the honest answer, and honestly, doesn't everybody think about hurting themselves sometimes?

So I said yes.

Then he started scribbling notes, saying he needed to refer me to a psychiatrist, and I said, aren't you a psychiatrist? And he said no, a psychologist, and I started freaking out thinking I'm so screwed up that a whole team is required to fix me.

And the next thing I know, I'm crying about Jamie shoplifting and ditching me at the mall, and how I keep hearing rumors about Chris seeing other girls but I don't believe the rumors because I totally trust Chris and I've never been happier in my life, and he and I just hung out at the lake last night and it was like magic.

But if I'm so happy, Dr. Deadhead said, why was I crying?

I said I didn't know ... maybe because he subtracted points from last week's visit because I didn't cry when I was supposed to.

Then our hour was almost up and I told him I couldn't see him next Monday because I'll be on a Beta Club trip, then the week after that I'll start cheerleading practice, plus Chris promised he'd take me camping (he'd better not break that promise for the fourth time, stinker!), then of course school starts back, and although I totally appreciate everything he's done for me, maybe it's time for me to stop talking about myself and just get on with my life.

He looked all concerned and said he would talk to Mom, but he thought we were making great progress and should continue.

Great progress? All I do during our sessions is cry (or get nailed for NOT crying when I'm supposed *to), and what good has all this crying done anyhow? And now I'm supposed to squeeze a psychiatrist into my schedule, too?*

I told Mom after my appointment that I wanted to be done with counseling, that I just wanted to get back to my life. She said we'd talk about it later.

But I suspect Mom is as ready to be done with Dr. Deadhead as I am.

Please Shannon, I think as I tuck the journal under my mattress for the night, *please don't be done with Dr. Deadhead. Please let him help you.*

Then I pull the journal back out and open it back to the entry I just read. My eyes lock on the date: *July 19, 1993.* God, I get so caught up in Shannon's journal that I almost forget her present is the past. *I suspect Mom is as ready to be done with Dr. Deadhead as I am.*

But she *is* almost done with Dr. Deadhead. She's almost done with everything.

Thirty-One

I'm almost finished."

Aunt Nic glances up at me from the work table. "Almost finished with the receipts?" she asks casually, tucking sprigs of baby's breath into a vase of red roses.

I shake my head. "Almost finished with Shannon's journal."

She catches my eye, puts down the baby's breath, then takes my hand. "Are you okay?"

I nod, my head dropping as my eyelashes flicker. "Just a few more pages to go. I guess I should just read it straight through at this point. But I don't want to be done." My throat catches.

Aunt Nic hugs me. "I'm sorry, honey," she says in a trembling voice. "I'm sorry this has been so hard for you. I really should never have given you that journal."

I shake my head as it rests on her shoulder. "I'm so glad you did. I feel like I know my sister now."

Aunt Nic pushes my shoulders back and looks at me squarely in the eye. "Just remember, honey. Like I told you before, the last summer of her life doesn't tell the whole story."

I nod. "I know. I totally get her. You know what's great? *She's* starting to get herself. You can read it in the journal—she's beginning to understand herself."

I squeeze my arms across my chest, shivering a little. "Everything I'm reading...it should be a beginning, not an end. I don't want to get to the end. I don't want *her* to get to the end."

Aunt Nic dabs her eyes. "I know, honey," she whispers. "I know."

"Life sucks, doesn't it?"

Aunt Nic smiles through her tears. *"Your* life is going to be amazing, sweetie. That would make Shannon so happy, to know her baby sister has such a bright future ahead of her."

I smile back at her.

Aunt Nic's eyes brighten. "Are you going to lunch with Gibs today?"

"Yeah. Just burgers."

"So when does your mom get to find out that you two are an item?" she asks mischievously.

"We're just friends," I tell her, but I blush when she looks at me knowingly.

"Just friends," I repeat, laughing as I say it.

Aunt Nic gives me a mock frown. "Well, if that's your story, I guess I'm sticking to it. But I don't know why you're being so secretive. Your mom thinks he's totally adorable, you know."

"Yeah, well, she's too old for him."

She laughs. "Just promise me I can sing at your wedding."

"Whatever," I mutter playfully. "As long as you throw in the flowers for free."

Thirty-Two

I stretch my arms, inhale deeply, and squint against the bleached-yellow sunshine pouring through my bedroom blinds on this lazy Sunday morning.

Eve texted me last night to remind me she's in town for a few days and make sure it's still okay for her and her mom to stop by later this afternoon. I said sure. I haven't exactly broken the news to Mom yet, but I'll cross this bridge when I come to it.

I reach under my mattress, pull out Shannon's journal once again, and open it to her next entry.

Tuesday, August 3, 1993

Can you say awkward?

Mom and I went shopping today with Eve and her mother, the whole mall run and food court

*extravaganza that we do every year before school
starts.*

I smile. That's the shopping trip Eve mentioned on the
phone. This entry is going to have a happy ending.

*Mom and Mrs. Brice go bananas over that disgusting
sweet-and-sour chicken. Tastes like grease balls
dunked in maple syrup that's passed its expiration
date.*
 *I remember how excited Eve and I used to get
about these shopping trips. She'd spend the night
before with me and we'd spend hours making a list.
Jelly bracelets or toe rings? Doc Martens or tennis
shoes? T-shirts or Polos? Power-shopping, we called it.*
 *So that was then. This is now. No sleepovers this
year, no lists. Just Mom and me meeting Eve and her
mom at the entrance of Macy's, followed by a bunch
of fake smiles and air kisses. Our moms dragged us
through the stores, up and down the aisles, with Eve
and me acting all fake-cheery but not even looking at
each other.*
 *Anyhow, we shopped for a couple of hours,
bought a few clothes, wolfed down some grease balls
in the food court and I thought, Thank heaven we're
done. Our shopping trips used to go on all day, but
every minute was dragging by like an hour. Even
Mom and Mrs. Brice seemed ready for this funfest to
be over.*

So … time to go, right?

Wrong.

Mom and Mrs. Brice suddenly announced they wanted to look at woks, or steamers, or something food-related. I said I'd come, too, but Mom said no, they'd just be a minute, Eve and I should just wait there in the food court.

So there we sat for the next half-hour. For the first few minutes, we stuck to safe conversation—how much reading would be involved in AP English, whether we'd have to do projects in honors chemistry, that sort of thing. I told her I was sorry I hadn't gotten to hang out with her much during the Beta Club trip, what with her being in Group A while I was in Group B.

Then, the weirdest thing happened. It was like we both got totally gushy at the same time.

She said, "I miss you, Shannon," and I said, "I miss you, too" and we were all sappy and blubbery, crying like babies.

I told Eve I was sorry we'd drifted apart, but I'd felt so judged by her, and she said no no no, she never meant to judge me, she just didn't want to see me get hurt. I told her that Chris and I are doing GREAT. She smiled and said she was glad to hear it, but she didn't look convinced. Whatever.

It just felt so good to feel close to her again. She and Chris will learn to love each other eventually. She'll come around when she sees for herself what a great guy he is. And she'll find a great guy of her own soon! I told her that would be our fall project.

Senior year, HERE WE COME!

P.S. I bit the bullet and kept my appointment with Dr. Deadhead yesterday. He said he was proud of me, that we'd come so far and that my future is so bright. And when I smiled, he said it was the first time he ever really saw me smile. A REAL smile. A GENUINE smile. A smile from the heart. I said, "What can I say? You bring it out in me."

I smile, thinking of Shannon and Eve hugging and crying in the food court at the mall.

Mom and Mrs. Brice must have done some behind-the-scenes plotting to make sure Shannon and Eve would have some time alone to patch things up. I guess Mom's micromanaging comes in handy once in a while. Once in a *great* while.

I finger the last few pages of Shannon's journal, the ones I have yet to read. After page upon page of angst and confusion, it's beyond exhilarating to read that, for one moment at least, she's excited about the future.

Senior year, HERE WE COME!

It occurs to me, just this instant, that *my* senior year is coming, too. I mean, of course I already knew that … but Shannon's journal has kind of disoriented me. I'm following her story so closely that I've lost track of my own.

I grin at her pep-squad verbiage and punctuation: *Senior year, HERE WE COME!*

"Senior year, here *I* come," I say aloud, feeling silly and wistful at the same time.

A knot clutches in my throat.

Oh, God, Shannon. I wish you'd had your senior year. I wish that so much.

But at least you were happy.

Except that she wasn't. Not for long. My stomach muscles tighten as I slowly turn the page, knowing I'm closing in on the last days of her life:

Saturday, August 7, 1993

Guess what I did tonight?

Go on ... guess.

Oh, forget it, you'd never figure it out.

I scrapbooked with Grandma! Isn't that the lamest thing you've ever heard?

But we actually had fun.

I was supposed to go to a party with Jamie, but I changed my mind at the last minute. The two of us hanging out always involves my car, my gas, my money, my jewelry for her to wear ... blah, blah, blah, blah, blah.

So when she asked if I wanted to go to some party and I said no, she was STUNNED. No? What would she do? How would she get there? Whose clothes would she "borrow"? (and forget to give back). Whose house would she sneak into and crash at? (since her folks lock her out if she's not home by her curfew, which she never is).

Of course, she couldn't say all those things, so instead, she tried to make me jealous. I'd better be there, she said, to keep an eye on my boyfriend.

Except Chris isn't even in town, I told her. He's at a car show with his dad.

That's what you think, she told me.

That's what I know, I told her.

But she kept trying to get me to change my mind. Why couldn't I go? What was I doing instead, knitting booties for orphans with my prissy friend Eve?

That didn't work either (and God, I'm so ashamed to think of the times when it did), so then Jamie started crying. She said I'm her best friend, her only friend, and I've been such a good example for her, and why oh why am I blowing her off?

The tears got to me. Okay, okay, I'll go, I told her. At first, she was gushing all over me—Thank you, thank you, you're my best friend ever!

But a few minutes later, she was calling me back with the same old snotty attitude, telling me which of my clothes she needed to "borrow" and how much money I needed to "lend" her.

So I told her I couldn't go after all. She was so mad she slammed down the phone.

And Grandma and I sat in the basement all evening, pasting family photos onto scrapbook paper and eating s'mores. Yes, she drove me crazy with her nitpicking, but what can I say? That's Grandma. At least she doesn't use me.

I'll never let myself be used again.

Thank God Shannon is seeing the light about Jamie. I turn to the next entry.

Tuesday, August 10, 1993

Something's up with Jamie.

She called this morning practically hyperventilating, telling me she needed to see me NOW. I lied and told her I was busy all day with a "family function." (Happy you taught me how to be such a good liar, Jamie?)

Tonight, then, she said.

Gee, sorry, I said. Busy tonight, too.

So she started up the waterworks again. She sobbed and blubbered and told me she has to see me, she just has to. She's got big news. HUGE. (Yawn.)

She sounded so frantic that I almost felt a little sorry for her. But when I think of how long I've let her call all the shots, I can't help but smile a little to see her squirm when the shoe's on the other foot.

I finally told her fine, I'd do my best to squeeze her in. So I guess I'll see her tomorrow.

Wonder what her big news is.

Okay, now *I'm* wondering, too. I turn the page to the next journal entry. I suck in a breath. Here I am, back to where I started.

Wednesday, August 11, 1993

I want to kill myself.

I take a deep breath. There are still a couple pages left. I'm not sure how this story will end—or whether Shannon will even *tell* me—but I know now that I don't want to find out alone.

I pick up my cell phone and call Gibs.

Thirty-Three

Gripping Shannon's journal, I go downstairs in my flannel pajama pants and T-shirt to wait for Gibs. I hover in the foyer for a minute, slipping the journal into my purse, then, too antsy to stand still, walk into the kitchen where Mom's kneading bread on the island counter.

"Hi, honey," she says without looking up.

I rush to the island and lean over the counter toward her, so close her that our noses almost touch. I have a sense of inevitability about whatever words are about to tumble from my mouth. There's no turning back now.

"Mom, was Shannon happy?" I ask in a quavery voice. "I mean ... toward the end. Was she happy?"

Mom freezes and looks at me accusingly.

"Why all this talk about Shannon lately? Why are you doing this to me, Summer?"

I fling my hands in the air, stymied. "Why does everything have to be about you? I'm asking about *Shannon*."

Mom's chin juts out. "How can it not be an indictment of me for you to insinuate Shannon wasn't happy? I was her *mother*." She puts a hand against her mouth. "I was a good mother," she adds bitterly. "And I'm a good mother to you, too. That doesn't mean I can make your life perfect. But it should be *enough*. It should be enough to give me some peace."

Her lower lip trembles, and she suddenly looks so small and vulnerable that I instinctively reach across the island to touch her. She holds up floury palms as stop signs.

"I have been very patient with you," she says through gritted teeth. "I realize you're the same age Shannon was when she died, and that you're bound to be curious about her. So, fine! Let's dig out some old photo albums. Let's watch some home movies. But don't suggest I was a bad mother to her, Summer. That's more than I can bear."

She sets her jaw and digs back into the bread dough, pounding and twisting it insistently.

"That's not what I meant, Mom. I never meant to..."

"I think this conversation is over," Mom says in a tight voice, still working the dough.

I shake my head slowly, then, before walking out in defeat, pound the kitchen counter with my fist, creating a floury cloud that quickly dissipates.

Mom doesn't seem to notice.

———

I run to Gibs' car in my driveway before he's even come to a stop.

He turns off the ignition as I climb into the passenger seat.

I exhale through an O in my mouth, staring straight ahead. "I think Shannon might have committed suicide."

He pauses and I turn to face him. "She says it, Gibs. I'm almost finished with the journal, and she says, *I want to kill myself.*"

Gibs' eyebrows widen.

"When I first got the journal?" I continue. "When I was thumbing through it? That's the first page I read. I've known since I started that I might find out her death was a suicide. Now I'm back to that page. Her journal is almost over—her *life* is almost over—and she's saying she wants to kill herself."

I start to cry, and Gibs clutches my hand.

"I don't want to keep reading," I tell him. "I don't want to know."

He loosens his grip, but keeps his fingers laced around mine. "But not knowing...all this speculation...nothing could be worse than that," he says. "Right?"

I shake my head. "Knowing would be worse. If I knew for sure that I could have had a sister in my life, but I don't because she did some stupid, cowardly thing for some stupid, immature reason...that would be worse."

The irony strikes me a beat too late. I would never have had a sister in my life. I remember what Gibs said when I first told him about Shannon: *If you were meant to be here, it's like Shannon had to die to make that happen.*

I cry softly as Gibs squeezes my hand tighter.

"I think you've got to have a little faith in your sister," he says.

I sniffle and rub my eyes. "Sometimes in her journal, she's so great, you know? Funny and real and perceptive. Then other times, she's this ridiculous, lovestruck little twit, the kind of girl I roll my eyes at in school. What if the twit came out on top at the end? What if she had some stupid drama-queen moment that she let define her life? That she killed herself over?" I lean my head against the headrest and gaze upward. "I just couldn't take it. I'd be so friggin' pissed at her. Then what would I do with all that frustration? Let it eat at me the rest of my life because she's not here to bawl out?"

Gibs smooths my hair. "Everything you're afraid of is what you're dealing with right now. Could knowing the worst be tougher than assuming the worst?"

I consider his words for a moment, turning my head and peering vacantly out the window.

Then I turn to him and nod sharply. "I'm going to finish her journal."

He smiles, his dark blue eyes incredibly kind and warm.

I inhale deeply, hold my breath for a second, then exhale. "Will you do it with me?"

He nods. "Let's go for it."

I pull the journal out of my purse and open it to her last entry.

Thirty-Four

Birds chirp and a nearby lawn mower whirs in the distance as I sit by Gibs in his car and read aloud:

Friday, August 13, 1993

"She died on August 16th," I tell Gibs somberly. "She wrote this three days before she died."

I start reading again:

I picked up my schedule today at school.

I glance at Gibs, alarmed. She goes from *I want to die* to *I picked up my schedule today at school?* I keep reading.

Everyone says junior year is the hardest, but I've got some killer courses coming up this year, all of them AP, which means projects, reports, essays—AARGH.

*It's okay, though. I'll take all the distractions
I can get. No use hashing out the gory details. I'm
sure everybody in town is already talking about it,
and I have so totally moved on that I really have
NOTHING to say on the subject, so ...*

ONWARD!

*I'm going to carpool with Evie, but I've got an
appointment with Dr. Deadhead right after school
Monday, so we'll drive separately the first day and
meet up in homeroom.*

I glance at Gibs again, but no words are necessary. *If
only Shannon had carpooled with Eve that day ... if only she
hadn't had an appointment with the shrink ... if only, if only,
if only ...*

*I think I'll wear my teal sweater to school Monday.
It's a little hot and itchy, but it's my eat-your-heart-
out sweater. Which is stupid, considering he won't
even be at school. But Jamie will.*

My eyes skitter away as I try to process the words. Then
they fall back on the journal.

They say living well is the best revenge.

*But you know what? I don't even want revenge.
Okay, maybe a little. But what I really want is
peace. I want my old life back, the one I had before
I started hanging out with them. I wish I could turn
back the clock.*

Or maybe I don't. My heart is crushed in a million pieces, but I'm wiser than I used to be. I feel like I lived most of my life like a china doll under glass. It was safe but it was boring.

That's one thing I can say—I certainly haven't been bored lately. Ha ha.

Well, my tears are back for the fortieth time today, and I absolutely REFUSE to have another sobfest, so I'm going jogging.

Mom doesn't know what's up, but she's acting all worried and hover-y (is that a word?), so I think I can squeeze another shopping trip out of her. (Smiley face.)

I don't mean to sound bratty, but what can I say. Shopping always cheers me up.

I finger the paper and bite my bottom lip. A quiet moment hangs in the air, then I flip through the last few empty pages of the journal to let Gibs know what I can't say out loud: that's it. Those are the last words Shannon wrote in her journal. She'll never again share another thought with me. I squeeze my eyes shut and press the journal against my chest.

"That's it," Gibs whispers, and I nod.

A neighbor's cat scampers around our rose bushes. The nearby lawn mower is still whirring. The hum of car engines drifts in and out of my consciousness—people going to church, going to the park, going on with their lives…

"You know now that she didn't commit suicide," Gibs says softly.

I glance at him. "You think?"

He nods. "It's obvious. She was all about the future. Whatever Chris and Jamie did to hurt her … she was moving on."

I nod, my eyes glistening with fresh tears. "I hope. But you know, she was so fickle and moody. By Monday, she could have been back in a funk."

Gibs shakes his head. "I don't think so. I think she sounds really strong."

My eyes soften. "She does, doesn't she?"

He nods. "She reminds me of you."

I smile at him as he takes my hand and presses it against his chest.

"Will you go with me on an errand?" I ask him. "I can't do it today because Eve and her mother are coming over later. But soon …"

"Sure. What's up?"

I take a deep breath. "I want to talk to Chris."

Thirty-Five

*W*ha..."

Mom's baffled expression lasts only a nanosecond, then is replaced by her trademark Hostess Smile.

I was counting on this. I'd pondered whether to tell her that Eve and her mother were coming over. But that would have led to questions and fretting and coffee cake–making, so I've opted just to let them show up on our doorstep, knowing that any emotions Mom might have will be trumped by social niceties.

"Oh, dear!" Mrs. Brice stammers. "Summer didn't tell you we were coming? Oh, Susanne, I'm so embarrassed!"

"No, no! Don't be ridiculous! Come in, come in!"

Mom is in full hostess mode now.

"No, really, Susanne, we don't need to stay. I just assumed

that Summer would…" Mrs. Brice casts an annoyed eye on me, but then softens it with a smile.

Mom is shuttling Eve and her mother toward our living room, swooping her arm in the general direction. A manicured fingernail directs them to our sofa. "Sit, sit!"

Mom and I sit in chairs as they settle onto the sofa.

"Well!" Mom says. "Heavens! How long has it been?"

Mrs. Brice's face falls. "Susanne, I just feel awful that I haven't kept in touch."

Eve nods, averting her pale blue eyes and pulling a strawberry-blond lock of hair behind her ear. Her lightly freckled face makes her look like a college kid.

"Nonsense!" Mom chirps. "Time just has a way of slipping away, doesn't it? But we're together now! That's what counts."

She claps her hands and turns toward Eve. "Evie! Tell me everything."

An awkward pause lingers.

Mrs. Brice clears her throat. "Susanne, you clearly weren't expecting us. I'm so sorry. I don't know what I was thinking, not calling first. Really, we just wanted to say hello, but we need to be going…"

Mom's smile stands at attention, like a drill sergeant has just blown a whistle. "You'll stay right where you are!" She gives a sharp nod. "I'm so sorry if I seem a little… confused. Summer has a way of springing surprises on me. But what a wonderful surprise this is! Honestly, having you drop by—it just makes my day!"

"Where's Mr. Stetson?" Eve asks.

"Where do you think?" Mom responds breezily. "Golf, of course! Some things never change. Evie, tell me how you've been doing. I know you're married. Three children, right?"

Eve looks like she wishes she could press an eject button, but she manages to smile back at Mom. "Uh … right. Two boys, eight and ten, and my baby girl. She's two." The smile is still pasted to her face, but her brows weave apologetically.

Mom fingers her pearls. "Little Evie, mother of three! And you're living in Charlotte?"

The eyes still look fretful. "Yes. Charlotte. My husband is in computers."

"Right!" Mom chirps. "You met him in college, right?"

Eve opens her mouth, but no words come. Her face crinkles like a leaf and her eyes flood with tears. "I should have invited you to the wedding." She gasps out a sob, then stuns us all by running to Mom and hugging her.

Mom's eyebrows arch, her smile still intact. She tries halfheartedly to stand, but Eve's weight is pressing her down. Mom casts nervous glances at Mrs. Brice and me.

"Evie, darling!" Mom's tone aims for sympathetic, but the edge is clear, as if a gunman is holding her hostage and she's trying to bring him to his senses while cajoling her way to safety.

Eve's sobs have turned into a freight train. Her whole body shakes as she clings tighter to Mom and weeps into her neck. Mom's expression grows increasingly frantic.

"Eve, honey…" Mrs. Brice says gently.

"No!" Eve protests with alarming conviction, her face still burrowed into Mom's neck. "I've wanted to hug you for so long, Mrs. Stetson! I'm sorry I couldn't bring myself to do it. I was so afraid I would cause you more pain. I'm so sorry about Shannon. I miss her so much."

Mom looks like she's drowning.

"Eve!" Mrs. Brice says firmly. "I know you're upset, honey, but poor Mrs. Stetson can't even breathe."

But Eve won't loosen her grip. Her back rises and falls to the cadence of her heaving sobs.

"I'm sorry," she weeps, sounding like a little girl. "I loved her, Mrs. Stetson. I love you, too."

I have to admit, I've taken in the whole scene with an anthropologist's sense of objectivity: Mom being swept up by a tsunami of emotion, Mom losing her grip on total control, Mom pinned to her seat, Mom's social niceties tested by her starkest of discomfort zones. My fascination knows no bounds.

But Eve's pain … it's so raw, so intense. As she continues to cry on Mom's shoulder and Mom begins to clumsily stroke her hair, I find my own eyes filling with tears. A sob lodges in my throat. I swallow hard, then notice that Mrs. Brice is crying, too. Her face is in her hands and her shoulders are trembling.

"Now, Eve, dear," Mom says. I know she doesn't intend to sound harsh, but her steady voice is so jarringly incongruous with our streams of tears that all eyes fall on her. She clears her throat and tries again. "I think what everyone needs is a nice cup of cocoa."

Eve pulls away and stares into Mom's eyes. Then … as if the past few moments haven't been weird enough … she laughs.

Mom looks at her, startled. Eve laughs some more … hearty, cathartic chuckles.

"We used to joke about that," Eve says, her face still so close she must feel Mom's breath on her cheeks.

"Wha…?"

"Shannon and I used to laugh about how you'd always try to make everything better with a nice cup of cocoa. No date to the prom? 'What you need is a cup of cocoa!' The dog devoured your science project? 'A cup of cocoa will do just the trick!' An asteroid destroys the Northern Hemisphere? 'Well, I'll just whip up a nice cup of cocoa!'"

Eve's eyes glisten and she laughs some more. She reaches out as if she wants to touch Mom's cheek, but she pulls back at the last moment.

Because now, Mom is crying.

I bite my lip. Confronting Mom with almost two decades' worth of pain and grief doesn't nudge her into vulnerability, but embarrassing her turns her to jelly.

"I didn't realize you made fun of me," she says in a brittle voice.

"Oh, Mrs. Stetson … no! No, Mrs. Stetson, that's not what I meant! We weren't making fun. We loved you for making everything better with your cocoa. Don't you see what a source of comfort that was for us?"

Mom waves a hand dismissively.

"Oh, Mrs. Stetson…" Eve continues plaintively.

Mom's hand is still waving. *Whatever, whatever…*

Damn her. Why is it so much easier for her to be cold than sad?

"You know what we called you?" Eve soldiers on.

Mom looks up at Eve, dampening her lashes as she blinks them against her tears.

"We called you Sue-nami. Sue, as in Susanne. You were such a force of nature. We were in awe."

We study Mom's face closely. This could go badly.

But Eve's sweet face is coaxing a smile from Mom's.

"Sue-nami? Like the storm?" Mom asks.

Eve nods, giggling through tears.

Then Mom starts giggling, too. Crying and laughing at the same time. Eve's fingers interlace with Mom's. Their knuckles turn white, they're squeezing so hard.

"You two weren't the only ones to come up with nicknames," Mom says, her teary eyes sparkling. "Remember when you and Shannon sprinkled bathroom bleach into the washing machine because we were out of laundry detergent?"

Laughter sputters from Eve's lips. "Shannon was Spic and I was Span!"

Mom laughs harder. "Your mom and I had to buy new cheerleading uniforms so our Red Devils wouldn't be pink!"

"Sixty bucks a pop!" Mrs. Brice interjects gleefully, laughing along with them.

"Oh, oh!" Eve says excitedly. "And don't forget how we almost set your kitchen on fire when we baked our first cake."

"'Bake' being the definitive word," Mom says in a playful-scolding voice. She looks over at me to deliver the punch line. "They broiled it!"

Eve is laughing so hard, she's teetering on her squatting feet.

"At least they didn't paint your kitchen!" Eve's mom says. "That was my Mother's Day surprise one year. Surprise! Your kitchen is pink!"

"To match our cheerleading uniforms," Eve says. Tears stream down their cheeks.

Dusk is settling in, and a gauzy peach ray of sun streams through the plantation shutters, making everyone's cheeks rosy.

"I never heard about the uniforms or the cake," I say softly.

Mom gazes at me warmly. "There were so many stories," she says. "Where do you begin?"

I don't know... at the beginning? In the middle? What the hell does it matter where you begin, just as long as you do? Oh, well. Maybe she's beginning now.

————

Mom and I are washing dishes when we hear the front door open.

"Anybody home?" Aunt Nicole calls from the foyer.

Mom glances over her shoulder. "Oh, by all means, let yourself in," she calls back. "Why stand on ceremony?"

Mom pokes me playfully in the side as I dry a porcelain teacup.

Aunt Nic joins us in the kitchen. "Dinner dishes?" she surmises.

"High tea," I correct her, curtsying. "We had guests."

She pulls a chair from the kitchen table and settles in. "Who?"

I reach for a soapy teacup that Mom has just finished washing, but she pulls it away from my grasp. "Go sit with Aunt Nicole," she tells me. "I'll finish up."

I sit next to Aunt Nic as Mom rubs a dishcloth against her china until it squeaks.

"Carole and Eve Brice came by," Mom says, attempting an oh-by-the-way tone.

Aunt Nic blinks hard. "You're kidding! Goodness, how many years has it been? How old is Eve now? She must be—what—in her mid-thirties?"

Silence.

Aunt Nic and I exchange puzzled glances, then look at Mom's back at the kitchen sink. *Squeak, squeak, squeak* goes the china.

"Sue?" Aunt Nic says.

More silence. *Squeak, squeak, squeak.*

Aunt Nic's eyes search mine for an explanation. I shrug.

"Mom, did you hear Aunt Nic?"

Squeak, squeak, squeak.

But then the squeaking stops. Mom freezes in her spot until her shoulders convulse. Her head drops and a sob rumbles through her throat.

"Sue...!"

Mom turns toward us, her blue eyes glistening with tears. The teacup in her hands drops to the ceramic tile, breaking into a thousand jagged pieces. Aunt Nic and I gasp and jump to our feet. Mom holds out a hand to stop us from coming closer.

"Stay where you are!" she says through her sobs. "You'll get cut."

We ignore her, rushing over and enveloping her in our arms.

"The glass!" Mom wails. "You'll cut yourself on the glass!"

"We don't care about the glass!" Aunt Nic says, pressing Mom's face into her neck.

"It'll cut you!" Mom insists, but we're not listening. We're just hugging her, Aunt Nic's fingers tangled with mine as we stroke Mom's hair.

"I have to clean it up," Mom says, but her voice is small now, defeated. She crumples into us, our muscles flexing to absorb her weight. Her sobs emanate from deep in her gut.

"It's okay," Aunt Nic whispers in her ear. "It's okay, Su-Su."

We stand there for a long time. Our faces turn sideways and rest on each other's shoulders. Our arms caress each other's backs.

"I miss my baby," Mom moans, then shakes as more sobs churn through her chest.

"I know," Aunt Nic coos. "I know."

"It's my fault," I say. "I shouldn't have called Eve. I didn't mean to upset you, Mom."

Mom's back suddenly stiffens and she pulls away from us. "Why *did* you call her?" she asks. I try to read her expression. Angry? Accusing? Betrayed?

I hold a hand against my mouth, grasping for words. "I don't know," I say, staring at the shattered glass on the floor. "I need to know her, Mom. You never talk about Shannon, other than superficial stuff. I want to know my sister. But I didn't mean to hurt you."

She takes my cheeks in her hands, her palms cool against my skin. "I'm glad you called her."

My face crumples. "But I made you cry."

Mom shakes her head. "It's okay to cry, sweet girl. My sweet baby girl," she says, and our tear-stained eyes stay locked for a long moment.

Then Mom's hand tugs self-consciously at the collar of her blouse. "I must look a fright," she says. "Let me go wash my face."

Broken glass crunches softly under her pumps as she starts to walk out of the room.

Aunt Nic suddenly smiles. "I can't believe it," she says. Mom turns around to see what she's talking about.

"This is the first time I've ever see you walk away from a mess," she tells her sister.

Mom blushes. "Oh, the glass!"

She starts rushing back into the kitchen, but Aunt Nic is shooing her away. "We're got it, we've got it," she assures her. Mom hesitates, then smiles and walks out of the room.

Aunt Nicole and I squat on the floor and gingerly start tossing pieces of glass into the wastebasket.

"Should I tell her?" I ask.

She looks at me quizzically.

"Should I tell Mom about the journal? Doesn't she deserve to know?"

Aunt Nic's eyes lock with mine. "I don't know what to tell you, honey. I'm sorry I've put you in such a tough spot."

I pluck more glass from the floor.

Suddenly, it doesn't feel like such a tough spot anymore.

Thirty-Six

"Can I help you?"

"Uh..."

I stare frantically at the plump brunette who has just opened the front door of her apartment to me, a baby in her arms. She's dressed in shorts and an oversized T-shirt. Her eyebrows seem locked into a perpetual V, making her look angry.

Even when she arches her brows (which she's doing now, prodding me to say something), the V stays in place.

God. Why didn't I anticipate somebody besides Chris answering the door?

"Um..." I say. "I'm looking for Chris Ferguson. Is he home?"

She narrows her eyes.

"He went to Chapel Heights High School, right?" I ask, pushing a lock of hair behind my ear.

"Yeah?"

"I'm a senior at Chapel Heights. Well, I will be in the fall. We're doing an alumni survey. I was hoping he might be willing to answer a few questions."

She tosses her head sideways.

"Chris!" she calls.

We stand there for a second, the baby reaching a pudgy hand in my direction.

"Chris!" the lady bellows again.

Jeez. The poor baby has to look at that scowl all the time.

I hear footsteps listlessly approaching the door.

Then I see him.

He gives me a blank stare. I pitch forward slightly, studying his face. He's got a slight paunch, dirty-blond hair, and a receding hairline. His features are even, and pleasant enough—I guess he had the potential to be good-looking a few years back. But now he just looks average, like the person you have to pass in a front office to get to the office of the person you're there to see. The kind of person nobody ever notices.

What the hell did Shannon see in him?

Now he's doing the eyebrow arch thing, waiting for an explanation.

The brunette turns and disappears into the apartment with the baby.

I take a deep breath. "I'm Shannon Stetson's sister."

The slightest hint of surprise flickers in his eyes. He stands silently for a moment, then closes the door as he joins me on the stoop, nudging me slightly backward in the process.

"What do you want?" he asks in a lowered voice.

He's towering over me. I didn't realize how tall he was until I could feel his breath on my face. My knees buckle slightly.

"You dated Shannon before she died ... right?"

He studies my face for a second, then nods almost imperceptibly.

"But you broke up?" I continue. "Right before she died?"

He holds a steady gaze. "Okay," he says evenly.

Whatever that means.

"Why did you break up?"

He rubs his chin. "Why are you here?"

"I just ... I don't know. She kept a journal before she died. I'm reading it. She writes about you."

His jaw tightens. I can tell that words are bouncing around in his head. "She was a nice girl." That's what he settles on. "I really don't have anything else to say."

I take a deep breath. "I'm meeting with Jamie later today." I blurt out this lie so quickly, I don't even remember forming it in my head.

Chris looks ... what? Mad? Panicked? "What the hell?" he says, rubbing his chin again. "Why are you dredging up all this crap?"

I've really got his attention now. "Jamie told me that ..."

"Jamie got pregnant on *purpose*."

My jaw drops for a nanosecond. I shut my mouth and suck in my bottom lip.

"Right," I say, trying to sound calm, almost bored even. "Shannon found out Jamie was pregnant, and then..."

"Jamie was always chasing after me," Chris says, spitting out his words. "She was nothing but a pest."

I bite the inside of my lip, willing my face to stay expressionless. I brush a windblown lock of hair out of my eyes.

"She faked being Shannon's friend so she could get to me," Chris continues, clenching his fists. "I told Shannon she was nothing but trouble."

"And yet... you and Jamie ended up getting together." It's the most benign way I can think to phrase it. I don't want to make him defensive.

"*One* time," Chris says, his eyes bulging. "*One* time I let my guard down. And that's all it took." He jams his hands in his pockets, his face reddening. He shakes his head slowly.

"Right. Then you told Shannon that Jamie was pregnant." I'm trying so hard to sound casual, you'd think we were discussing the weather.

Chris' eyes flicker at me. "Jamie told her," he mutters, the indignation still fresh in his voice. "Shannon would never speak to me again."

I swallow hard. "So then, Jamie had the baby and..."

A vein in his neck throbs. "She told you she had my kid?"

"Um…"

Chris eyes me suspiciously. "What did Jamie tell you?"

I feel my face flush. "Nothing…nothing. I haven't talked to her yet. We're meeting later today, remember?"

He shakes a finger at me. "Well, don't believe anything she says. That psycho is a liar."

I glance at him anxiously. "So she didn't have the baby."

He eyes me suspiciously. "Are you playing some kind of game with me?"

Damn. I fold my elbows across my chest, shift my weight, and stare at my sneakers. "No, I just…"

"Look. I don't know what you know and what you don't know, or why the hell you're showing up on my doorstep, but I've said all I'm going to say." He turns to open the front door.

"Wait…" My eyes fill with tears. "Did you love her?" I ask, and he stops in his tracks.

"Did I love Jamie?"

My jaw drops again. "No. Shannon. Did you love Shannon?"

My sister, you moron.

He shrugs. "Shannon? Yeah."

Oh God. He might as well be commenting on his favorite football team.

I clamp my teeth together. "Because she loved you, you know."

His eyes fall.

"*She loved you,*" I repeat, my voice trembling.

He scratches the back of his neck. "Yeah." He looks puzzled. "We were kids, you know?"

This imbecile. This stupid clod that Shannon wanted to marry, to spend the rest of her life with, was screwing her best friend behind her back and dismissing Shannon as casually as if she'd been a girl behind a counter serving him ice cream.

"Did you even go to her funeral?" I suck in my bottom lip to steady it.

Anger flashes across his face, but then his expression softens. "It tore me up when she died," he mutters. "Especially since I never got a chance to explain..." He sighs. "I guess there was nothing *to* explain. I was a jerk. But I was sorry. I wish she'd let me tell her I was sorry."

A tear rolls down my cheek and I take a deep breath. "Do you think she hit that tree on purpose?"

His shoulders stiffen. "On purpose? You mean, because of...?"

He can't even comprehend it—being heartbroken enough, betrayed enough, to want to die.

"*No,*" he says emphatically, but it's obvious he was considering the possibility for the first time. Bastard. Did he even lose a single night's sleep over Shannon's death?

I hug my arms tighter across my chest, shivering in the humid ninety-degree heat. What do I want from him? A lifetime of teeth-gnashing?

I don't know. But I can't bear him reducing Shannon to a fling, an afterthought.

"I wish I'd been here to protect my sister from guys like you."

Chris plants a hand on his hip and wags his finger at me again. "Like I said, I don't know why you showed up on my doorstep, but the past is the past. That's it."

He turns around, flings his front door open with a flourish, and slams it shut behind him.

That's it.

———

The rubber soles of my sneakers pad down the concrete apartment steps. *Thud, thud, thud.* I reach the landing and run toward Gibs' car in the parking lot.

He gets out of the driver's seat as I approach him. I fall into his arms, crying.

"Bastard. *Bastard*," I mutter.

"What did he say?" Gibs asks, pulling my shoulders back so he can study my face.

I shake my head, squeezing tears out of my eyes. "She was nothing to him. A fling! It never even crossed his mind that she might have wrecked her car on purpose."

"He said that?"

I nod. "Among other things. Remember Jamie, the 'best friend'?"

Gibs' eyes prod me on.

"He got her pregnant. Chris got her pregnant! That's what Shannon was so upset about."

Gibs exhales slowly.

"It was just another summer vacation to him," I say bitterly. "Shannon was nothing but some cute girl to hook up with. As long as he got what he wanted from her, he was happy enough. Then, when he got bored...on to the next girl."

Gibs interlaces his fingers with mine. "I think that's all that most guys are capable of at this age."

I shake my head. "Why couldn't she have met someone like you?"

His dark blue eyes look so kind. Usually he looks down when I compliment him, but this time, his eyes stay locked with mine. "Thank you," he says softly.

A breeze ripples through my hair. "She wanted to marry him," I say, rolling my eyes at the stupidity of it all. "Shannon was so smart, but she wanted to spend the rest of her life with this stupid, shallow guy. If only she'd listened to Mom."

Gibs studies me closely, then the slightest of smiles creeps across his lips.

I drop my head and laugh. I'm as stunned as he is at what I've just said.

Thirty-Seven

"Excuse me..."

I hadn't planned on stopping by Mr. Kibbits'
classroom. It's registration day at school and I've come to
the cafeteria to pick up my schedule. It was while I was
standing in the *N-Z* line, smiling nonchalantly at familiar
faces as they milled around the room, that I decided to
pop my head into his room. I'm glad I haven't thought it
through. I have no idea what I'm going to say to him. I'm
not even sure he's here.

But he is.

"Summer!" he says brightly, looking up from his desk
as he sees me hovering in the doorway. His gray hair looks
freshly trimmed, framing his boyish face. His tie is loosened.

"Come in, come in!" he adds, glancing at the piece of paper I'm holding. "A problem with your schedule?"

I shake my head.

He smiles. "I didn't think so. Come sit down."

He nods toward a chair by his desk, then stands up and waves me toward it.

I sit down as he gathers the papers on his desk into a stack and moves them aside. He crosses his arms, leans back casually, and looks me in the eye.

"So. How are you doing?"

I tug a lock of hair. "Okay. I just wanted to say hi."

He pauses, studying my face. "Have you finished Shannon's journal?"

My eyes fall, and I stare at my fingers. "*She* didn't finish it," I say softly. "Life just ... left her hanging, you know?"

He pauses, then nods. "I guess that's what ultimately happens to everybody. We're here one day, gone the next." He clears his throat. "I didn't mean to sound insensitive," he qualifies.

"It's okay," I insist. "I know it's a bummer she died so young, but I'm kinda getting that. We're here one day, we're gone the next, and life goes on."

I steal a glance at him. "Did you know her boyfriend got her best friend pregnant?"

Mr. Kibbits blushes and looks at his lap. "There were rumors."

"Did Jamie have the baby?"

He tugs at the knot in his tie. "No. She was in school that fall."

"An abortion?"

He blushes again. "I don't know, Summer. Maybe a miscarriage. I never knew Jamie very well, and I think she dropped out before she graduated. But she was in school most of the year, and she obviously wasn't pregnant. For whatever reason, her pregnancy didn't last long."

"And Chris?" I persist. "Did she and Chris stay together?"

He shakes his head vigorously. "I don't think they were ever together."

Of course. She was just having his baby, that's all. Jamie meant nothing to Chris. For the first time, I feel a stab of pity toward her.

I take a deep breath, then look into his eyes. "Do you think Shannon drove into that tree on purpose?"

I can tell that Mr. Kibbits wants to look away, but he forces himself to hold my gaze. I hear the ticking of his clock as a few seconds pass.

"No," he finally says in a firm voice. "Shannon was a very smart, sensible girl. She had her whole life ahead of her." He pauses. "She didn't ... imply anything like that in her journal, did she?"

I clutch my schedule tighter. "She found out right before she died that Jamie was pregnant. She was really upset."

Mr. Kibbits' eyebrows weave together.

"But a couple of days after she found out, she wrote about going to school to pick up her schedule ... just like I'm doing now," I continue. "I'm sure she was still upset, but the entry was ... I don't know ... matter-of-fact."

The clock ticks away more seconds.

"She wouldn't have picked up her schedule, she wouldn't have seemed so matter-of-fact, if she was planning to ..." My voice drifts away.

Mr. Kibbits nods quickly, as if he's convincing himself at the same time he's trying to convince me. "Right. She was moving on."

"That was her last journal entry," I say. "The Wednesday of that week is when she found out about Jamie. She wrote, *I want to kill myself.* But then, two days later, she's writing about picking up her schedule, what classes she's taking, planning to carpool with Eve. Did you see her any of that week? The days before she died?"

"No," he says quietly. "I wish I had. I didn't know she was going through such a hard time. About all that, anyway. The rumors about Jamie didn't get cranked up until school was back in session, so ... I didn't know. I wish I'd been able to help her."

My eyes flicker toward his. "I know about my dad now."

He studies my face for a second.

"I'm sorry," he says.

I finger my chin. "All her illusions evaporated that summer," I say, more to myself than to him. "She found out about Dad's affair, she realized Mom was all about appearances, she got her heart broken ..."

Mr. Kibbits picks up a pencil and taps it against his desk, the rhythm jarringly dissonant with the ticking of the clock. "Life's never that cut and dried," he says. "Shannon had some problems, but she was working through them. If she'd lived longer, she would've had *new* problems, then worked through those. Like all of us do." He lets the pencil drop from his grasp. "That's life."

He leans closer toward me. "I'm sorry you had to learn about the turmoil she was going through. I'm sorry she had some tough breaks before she died. But her life wasn't about turmoil and tough breaks, Summer. I knew her. Trust me—she was happy."

I hug my arms together. "As best as I can tell, her life never had many tough breaks before that summer. Maybe it was too much for her. Maybe she didn't want to live unless her life could be perfect. Maybe she didn't think she *deserved* to live if her life wasn't perfect."

Tick. Tick. Tick.

"You know what I think?" Mr. Kibbits says in a far-away voice, fingering his pencil again. "I think she was growing up that summer, getting wiser and stronger. I think she would have made a hell of a grown-up."

Tick. Tick. Tick.

"I wish I could have helped her," I say.

Mr. Kibbits smiles at me. "She would have wanted to help *you.*"

I swallow hard to tamp down the knot in my throat. I squeeze my eyes shut, and when they open, they fall on the schedule I'm holding in my lap...

1st period: Spanish II, rm. 108, Dawson
2nd period: English Composition, rm. 222, Brantley

3rd period: Sociology, rm. 206, Parkinson
4th period: Lunch
5th period: Anatomy, rm. 417, Raleigh
6th period: Gen. Statistics, rm. 303, Portman
7th period: Study Hall, rm. 136, Bell

I glance up at Mr. Kibbits.

"Here's my schedule," I say, handing it to him. "Wanna take a look and give me the inside scoop on my teachers?"

His face brightens. He takes my schedule and feigns a look of intense concern.

"My God, you'd be better off getting taught by monkeys."

We laugh.

"Kidding," he says. "Although Mrs. Parkinson *is* a little on the boring side. The word in the teachers' lounge is that several students have actually lapsed into comas during her class. But you didn't hear it from me."

He hands me back my schedule and we smile.

"Sorry I can't be in your English class," I tell him. "AP classes are a little out of my league."

He taps his pencil on the desk again. Now, it's in synch with the ticking of the clock.

"I'm sorry, too. I don't think you have a clue how much you're capable of. But you'll find out."

I nod. "Thanks for talking to me," I tell him.

He nods back, then holds up an index finger. "You know ... a teacher's recommendation is all it would take to transfer you from College-Prep English to AP Comp," he says. "And if *I* happened to be the teacher to make the rec-ommendation, then I could pretty much guarantee which AP Comp class you'd end up in."

I blush and smile.

"Push yourself a little, Summer," Mr. Kibbits says. "I think you'd do a great job in my class. What do you say?"

I shrug. "I think I'd love your class."

He nods. "Then it's a done deal. But rest up this week-end. I'll work you pretty hard."

I smile. "I think I'm up for it."

He smiles back. "I think so, too."

I whisk a lock of hair off my shoulder. "Thanks. Really."

"You're welcome. Really. I think you're going to have a wonderful year."

I smile and stand up. I reach out to shake his hand, then feel vaguely self-conscious. A handshake? When the hell did I start shaking people's hands?

But Mr. Kibbits takes my hand and embraces it warmly.

"You're going to have a great year," he repeats.

And, just like that, I believe him.

Thirty-Eight

I think I've found her."

I pull the front door closed behind me and join Gibs on the front porch. My parents and I finished dinner an hour ago, but the scent of pork chops still drifts in the air.

"Found who?" I ask.

He motions with a nod, and I follow him to the porch steps. He sits on the top one, pulling a piece of paper out of his jeans pocket.

I peer at it. It's a printout of a web page … a page full of addresses.

"A list of the Jamie Williamses within a hundred-mile radius," Gibs explains.

"Oh," I say. "Hey, guess what? I stopped by to see Mr. Kibbits today when I was picking up my school schedule. He said he could get me into his AP Comp class next year."

Gibs looks confused, then smiles. "Good. That's exactly where you should be. So anyway, I was surfing the Net for..."

"Unfortunately, I got Parkinson for sociology," I continue. "But, man, I'm stoked about Mr. Kibbits' class. A hell of a time for me to have honors aspirations, huh?"

Gibs' head inches closer to mine as he gazes at me quizzically. "O-*kay*," he say. "Anyway, Jamie Williams is a really common name, but I narrowed down..."

I hold up the palm of my hand.

"*What?*" Gibs asks, more confused than ever.

"What classes are you taking?" I ask him.

"What *what?* Classes? I dunno... the schedule's in my car. I'll show it to you later. Anyway, of the several dozen Jamie Williamses within a hundred-mile radius—you figure the Jamies of the world never venture too far from home—I found three who—"

My hand shoots up again.

Gibs squeezes his eyes shut for a second. "*What?*" he asks again, confusion tinged with irritation.

I gently pull a strand of hair away from his face. "Thank you," I say sincerely. "Thank you for trying to track her down."

His eyebrows arch. "*But...?*"

"But I don't think I want to find her."

A squirrel scampers across the lime-green lawn, darting nimbly through Mom's impatiens and climbing a tree. A red bird on a branch of the tree squawks disapprovingly, spreads its wings, and soars into the sky.

I take the paper from Gibs' hands, fold it, and set it aside. "I don't think I could take it if I tracked down Jamie and she reacted the same way Chris did, almost like, 'Shannon *who*?'" I stare at my hands. "I don't know what I was expecting. I mean, I know they were 'just kids' and all, but Shannon has always been larger than life to me, and to have her reduced to that dumb blank stare on Chris' face…Besides, Jamie wasn't a real friend. She was just a blip in Shannon's life."

Gibs rubs his chin. "But she's the one who told Shannon she was pregnant. She could tell you things that…"

I fan another mosquito away from my face, then lean back against the porch on my elbows.

"I don't think it makes sense to try to turn Shannon's life into some deep, dark mystery," I say, peering at the lightning bugs that have begun blinking through the evening breeze. Or maybe they've been in the air all along, and it's only just now, when the dusk is descending like a curtain, that I'm able to see the flashes of light. "I know what I need to know. I think it's time to move on."

Gibs considers my words, then nods sharply. "Good plan."

I smile as I study his face closer. "You know," I say playfully, "I can't help thinking that although Shannon totally outshone me in pretty much every area of life, I have infinitely better taste in boyfriends."

He angles his face and brings it closer to mine. My face presses toward his and we kiss. My hands wrap around the back of his neck. Crickets chirp louder as we push closer and closer together.

Beep!

We glance up, startled. Aunt Nic has just pulled into the driveway. She waves at us heartily as she gets out of the car.

"Don't stop on my account," she calls, walking toward us.

Gibs jumps to his feet. "Hi..."

"Hi, Gibson," Aunt Nic says. "Don't get up. I was just in the neighborhood and thought I'd bring Summer her paycheck." She winks at me and I drop my face into my hands.

"I was just leaving..." Gibs stammers.

"You don't have to."

"No, really," he insists. "I have to be getting home." He gives me a formal little nod. "Summer. And Mrs...."

"Call me Nicole, remember?" Aunt Nic tells him. "Or Nic. Nic is good."

He swallows hard. "Alright then. Goodbye, Mrs.... Goodbye."

Gibs drops his head and rushes down the steps. I giggle and wave as he gets into his car and drives off.

Aunt Nic looks at me and mouths, "Oh my God!" She joins me on the stoop. "You little sneak... you *are* a couple! Like, duh. I *knew* it."

I laugh and twirl a piece of hair around my finger.

"He's adorable, by the way," Aunt Nic adds.

I wrinkle my nose. "You think?"

"Uh, totally. Have you told your mom yet that you two are an item?"

I roll my eyes. *"Item,"* I repeat mockingly, making Aunt Nic laugh. "Mom is on a need-to-know basis only. You'll keep quiet under penalty of death."

"Why?" she asks with an exaggerated pout. "Your mom would be thrilled. She'd be inviting Gibson over for dinner, and packing picnic lunches for the two of you, and taking his mother to lunch, and—"

"Yeah, that's kinda why."

"Well, you'd better stop smooching on the front porch, or the jig will definitely be up."

We smile as a warm breeze gently buffets our hair.

"I finished her journal," I say softly.

Aunt Nic lays her hand on my back. "Are you glad you read it?"

I nod. The lightning bugs are in full swing now, dancing through the air like neon confetti. "Did you know she'd broken up with Chris right before she died?"

"Mmmm," Aunt Nic says. "Your mom told me. She didn't have many details—she was just so happy Shannon had finally seen the light."

"So you didn't talk to Shannon about the breakup?" I ask cautiously.

Aunt Nic shakes her head. "I wish I had. Uncle Matt and I were at the beach the week before she died. We got home late that Sunday night, then, the next morning..."

I take a deep breath of honeysuckle-scented air. "It was

nice to find out that Shannon wasn't perfect. Makes me feel a little less hopelessly disappointing."

Aunt Nic rubs my back. "Why would you think that?" she asks. "You're the bravest person I know. That's why I trusted you with Shannon's journal."

I smile at her. "Thanks. I think I'll trust Mom and Dad with it."

She pauses, then nods, her eyes warm.

"They can read it if they like, or put it away ... whatever," I say. "But it should be their choice to make. I know some of it might freak them out, but ... I think Shannon got the fundamental flaw in our family."

"Yes?" Aunt Nic prods.

"That what we have here," I say, in my best *Cool Hand Luke* imitation, sweeping my arm toward our house, "is a failure to communicate."

Aunt Nic giggles.

I giggle, too, then rest my chin on my hand. "I don't want to fail at communication any more," I say.

Aunt Nic takes a deep breath. "Well," she says, the crickets chirping in the background, "I think you and Shannon make a pretty good team."

Thirty-Nine

I walk into the house, the garlic scent from the pork chops still lingering in the air. I pass Mom scrubbing pots in the kitchen and wave at her casually, then go into the den. The news is on TV and Dad is sitting at the computer.

"Hi, Dad," I say.

"Hi, hon."

I sit in the swivel chair and turn in his direction. Dad turns around and faces me.

"Can I ask you a question?" I say.

He smiles. "Shoot."

I tilt my head a bit. "How did you and Mom deal with it when Shannon died?"

He looks a little startled, then runs his fingers through his hair. "Your mother kept me going. She kept *us* going. I couldn't have gotten through it without her."

I search his eyes.

"You're like your mother," he tells me. "Strong. And smart."

A sudden whoosh of Shalimar fills the air. Dad and I glance toward the door and watch Mom walk in.

"Summer, I forgot to ask you during dinner—did you remember to pick up your schedule from school?"

I nod. "I'm all set. Ready to start senior year Monday."

My eyes dart from one parent to the other to gauge their reactions. Dad looks wistful; Mom looks unflappable. She starts rifling through mail.

I steel myself and keep going. "I'm about to catch up with Shannon," I say. "That's the last thing she ever did. Start the first day of her senior year."

Mom and Dad exchange glances, then Mom looks at me with a sense of urgency. "Summer, you're going to be *fine*," she says decisively. "You're going to go to school Monday and have a wonderful day. Then you're going to have a wonderful year. Then you're going to get on with the rest of your life."

I nod. "I know. I'm not superstitious or anything. I know it'll be just another day. But ... I've been thinking about Shannon a lot lately." I look at Mom steadily. "Tell me about the last weekend of her life," I say gently. "Right where we are today: the weekend before the senior year of high school. What was her last weekend like?"

Mom's jaw drops slightly. The pendulum on the mahogany grandfather clock ticks dully.

"Please tell me," I plead. "If I know, I won't wonder."

Mom bright-blue eyes widen. They're suddenly moist. Dad intertwines his fingers.

"There was nothing remarkable about that weekend," Mom says, staring out the window. "Shannon was a little down. She'd had a crush over the summer on some boy..." Her lip curls. "I think, by the end of the summer, she realized it was just infatuation. But still... it was hard for her."

"Did she talk to you about it?" I prod.

"Do *you* talk to me about those sorts of things?" Mom asks defensively. "Teenagers don't talk to their mothers."

"She talked to me."

Dad's voice is so small, we barely hear the words. But our eyes fall on him immediately. "She talked to me about him," he repeats.

I lean in closer. "What did she say?"

He opens his mouth, but closes it. Then he opens it again... and a sob rushes out.

I lean in to hug him. He grips me so hard, I wonder if my ribs will break.

"Randall," Mom says, but her voice is kind.

"She was in love with him," Dad says through his tears, still holding me close.

"She wasn't in *love*..." Mom protests.

"She was in love," Dad repeats. "I tried to warn her, but she was... she was a kid. He broke her heart, of course. She cried her eyes out to me, right before she died."

"What did you tell her?" I ask.

"I told her I was sorry, that she deserved better. That he was nothing, that she'd have a million more boyfriends."

He sobs openly now. Mom's face crinkles like a leaf. The mail drops from her fingers and her hands shake.

"It was nothing," she insists, weeping. "It was just a silly little crush."

"It wasn't nothing," Dad says firmly, pulling away from me and rubbing his fists roughly against his cheeks. "It wasn't nothing."

A long moment hangs in the air.

"Still," Dad finally says, his voice steadier now, "she was okay. She was getting through it. I told her she should go shopping with her mother. Shopping always cheered her up."

Mom walks toward us. "She bought four pairs of shoes," she says, smiling through her tears. "It was ridiculously extravagant, but we decided we could both wear the shoes, so what the heck. We had the same shoe size."

Mom stoops at the foot of my chair. Dad looks at her tenderly. "Those shoes are still in the boxes in my closet," she says.

"Shannon and your mother were very close," Dad tells me.

Mom smiles wanly through her tears. "She was tough on me," she says. "Like you are, Summer. She kept me on my toes. She hadn't always been that way—just toward the end. She was suddenly questioning everything, making me justify everything I said or did. It was exhausting."

She laughs lightly, and Dad and I smile at her.

"My girls have really managed to put me in my place," she says, reaching over and placing a cool palm against my cheek.

"We love you," I say, then blush self-consciously. "*I* love you. I know Shannon did, too."

Mom's face crinkles again. "She *did*," she says emphatically. "She *did* love me. Both of my babies love me."

I nod. "How could we not? You're so damn lovable."

Laughter sputters through Mom's lips, then Dad and I join in, all of us laughing through our tears.

"Hey, guess what," I say after a few moments, gazing at their rosy cheeks and bright, moist eyes. "Gibs and I are...let's see, what lame term did Aunt Nic use? We're an item."

Mom's eyebrows shoot up. "Oh, so we're confiding in Mommy now, are we!"

I love the sparkle in her eyes. "I guess we are. But don't start picking out china patterns or anything. Play it cool, Mom. Please."

She swats me playfully on the leg. "I've been playing it cool all summer! You think a mother doesn't know these things?"

I pause and glance at Shannon's watercolor portrait on the wall. Her hair is windblown in the image, her white cotton dress blowing, her feet bare on a sandy shore as waves lap at her ankles.

"I don't want to keep secrets," I say softly, then swallow hard and continue. "There's something I'd like you guys to see..."

Nicole Renee Photography

About the Author

Christine Hurley Deriso is the award-winning author of three middle grade novels. She has also contributed to *Ladies' Home Journal*, *Parents*, and other national magazines. Visit her online at www.christinehurleyderiso.com.

Where did the idea for *Then I Met My Sister* come from?

I wanted to explore the idea of connectivity ... that we're all linked to both the past and the future in ways that defy time or space. I never knew my ancestors, but I'm intrigued about how the seeds they cast long ago are influencing my life today. Likewise, I wonder how the choices I'm making will affect my descendants. I was intrigued by the concept of Summer reaching into her past to shape her future.

I also wanted to explore relationships that resonate strongly with me. I'm a mother, a daughter, and a sister, and I love the complexities and nuances of those roles. I like trying to see behind the façade of people's personalities and understanding the insecurities and vulnerabilities that lie beneath the surface. For instance, perfectionist control-freak Susanne seems so easy to dislike until you peel away the layers. I loved the challenge of trying to make her lovable, or at least understandable. I think books can do that better than any other art form: remind us of our shared humanity, our shared frailties, and inspire a bit of insight and compassion.

I was also interested in exploring the life of an average teen. Teenage years have always been challenging, but life for today's teens seems almost unbearably stressful. I know it's important to plan for the future, but our society seems to give teens no room at all to live for the moment, to appreciate the present as a gift in its own right rather than as a stepping stone to the future. It's stripped a lot of spontaneity and joy from teens' lives, and I think that's really sad.

I want teens to trust their wisdom, their bravery, their insight, and their instincts. I want them to explore what they want from life, rather than what others (like Summer's momzilla mom) are thrusting on them. But mostly I want them to have a sense of humor … to be able to step back and laugh at the absurdities of life and know that this, too, shall pass. I want them to recognize the universality in the human condition and to have compassion for everyone they encounter. I want them to be joyful. I want them to lose themselves in a good book, and to learn about themselves in the process. That's why I wrote this book.

Summer's got a very … interesting relationship with her family. What was your family like as a teen?

I'm the fourth of five children, and like Summer, I was intimidated by the standard set by my older siblings. They were very high-achieving, and by the time I was in high school, I'd settled into academic mediocrity, masking my insecurity as non-conformity. Thank heaven my parents took it in stride, because I'm not sure I could have mastered calculus under the best of circumstances.

In fact, my mom was the *anti*-momzilla. She's unconditionally loving, very open-minded, and whole-heartedly accepting of my choices. She never used guilt or manipulation to try to get her way. When I wrote the character of Summer's control-freak mother, Susanne, I thought, "What would Mom do?" Then Susanne would do the opposite.

My parents are also extremely bright, well-read, and creative, so my teenage years were filled with lots of music, books, and interesting dinner conversation. Mom wrote poetry, Dad wrote songs, and we all tended to follow their lead of creativity and self-expression.

Maybe it was because my family was such a tight unit that I was a pretty introverted teen. I spent a lot of time reading and playing my guitar. I had a few close friends, but I hated forced fun, like parties. I wish I'd nudged myself a little more out of my comfort zone than I did, but I always sensed my best days were ahead, and I just wasn't very interested in typical teenage stuff. Proms? Whatever. I had the great American novel to write! (I hadn't quite mastered the finer points of modesty at that point.)

In the book, Summer is raised with a very different idea of who her sister was than the one she comes to find in the diary. Have you ever found your perception of someone challenged and been forced to change your view?

Definitely, both for better and for worse. We've all been disillusioned by public figures who have fallen from grace, for instance, and I think every example is a cautionary tale that we shouldn't put people on pedestals. We're all human and we all have the potential for the full range of human behavior. The better we understand that, both about others and about ourselves, the more compassion and insight we can bring to our relationships.

Of course, one of the great joys in life is changing your view of someone else for the *better*. That's happened in my life too many times to count. When I was younger, for instance, my own insecurities led me to equate popularity with superficiality, or self-confidence with snobbishness. I wonder how many relationships I cut off at the pass with these silly assumptions.

The older I get, the more I realize how unreliable impressions can be. The jerk who cuts you off in traffic, for instance, may have just come from a doctor's appointment with a cancer diagnosis. You just never know what people are going through. I hope as I've gotten older, I've grown more understanding and compassionate.

If you had been in Summer's shoes, would you have had the courage to read the diary?

I think I would have had the courage to read it, but I wouldn't have had the courage to make the choice she makes at the end of the book. Like Summer, I tend to be pretty guarded, yet somehow assume people know what I'm thinking. My excellent and insightful Flux editor spotted that right away when he read the first draft of the novel. "Let us into Summer's head more," he'd tell me. "We need to know what she's thinking."

I thought, "What's he talking about?" For instance, in my mind, Summer was *clearly* in love with Gibs; it went without saying ... didn't it? Uh ... no, it didn't. Forcing myself to reveal more of Summer was forcing myself to reveal more of myself to the reader. It felt like therapy ... scary, but ultimately very liberating and cathartic.

In guiding Summer to strip away layers of secrecy and duplicity, leading to the denouement of sharing the journal with her parents, I became braver and more self-revelatory myself. I wish I'd learned Summer's lessons earlier in my own life.

As a writer and as a reader, what types of stories interest you?

Authenticity is key. If a character's voice doesn't ring true, I'm not interested in reading further.

I also like witty dialogue. I love Scout's irreverence and insouciance in *To Kill a Mockingbird*, the timeless charm of Mark Twain's characters, and the sardonic edge of a writer like David Sedaris.

Imagination gets high marks from me as well. I've incorporated the supernatural into a couple of my novels because ... well, in fiction, you can do whatever you want, so why not? I like being surprised and transported. For instance, I was gripped by the creepiness of Kazuo Ishiguro's *Never Let Me Go*.

I also value bravery in books. Writing can be like therapy. The more honest it is, the more it will resonate with readers. What teen can't identify with Holden Caulfield in *The Catcher in the Rye*? What dysfunctional family can't relate to Mary Karr's *The Liars' Club*? The best writers never flinch.

Life lessons are fine in stories, but they should seduce the reader, not club him over the head. If a dose of nobility sneaks up on a reader, great, but it should never be at the expense of authentic writing or great storytelling. I hate preachiness and self-righteousness. We *all* have lessons to learn, and the more honest a writer is, the more evident that is. A writer's agenda shouldn't be to impart a lesson; it should be to let wisdom reveal itself naturally in the course of great storytelling.